The Sheikh's Runaway Bride
Mel Teshco

GW00499978

Chapter One

Newly married bride, Sheikha Arabelle Al Qantisi, slowed the car at the crossroads, her gritty eyes searching Rajhabi's desert landscape for recognizable signs. A pity arriving yesterday morning in a helicopter at her soon-to-be-husband's palace meant she didn't have much to go on.

Add in the sandstorm, which had given her the opportunity to escape from her sheikh husband, but which had also reformed half the landscape, and her navigation was seriously messed up.

She shivered. Despite Sheikh Mahindar Al Qantisi's western education, he was steeped in tradition and would be furious at his runaway bride. If she was caught she would be severely reprimanded and would no doubt be made an example of in front of his people.

She glanced into the rearview mirror at the dust trail forming on the long road behind. Swallowing a gasp, she turned right and accelerated hard. She'd do whatever had to be done before she allowed Mahindar to capture her.

Her lips thinned. He might have put on a pleasant façade and pretended to be a loving husband to his wife, but theirs was nothing more than an arranged marriage. A farce. She had no doubt once he did his duty and impregnated her, he'd return to the pampered arms of his women.

That he still kept a harem spoke volumes about her husband.

"Ugh!" She might be born a sheikha but she'd had a western education, too, and despite living in a strict UK boarding school, she'd sampled far more freedom there than what she'd ever had in her homeland.

She'd never tolerate oppression again.

Her tyrant father, Sheikh Abdul Al Hussam, ruler of Lumana in the most western region of the United Arab Emirates, had only allowed her a UK education to get her out of his sight. His eldest child and only son had been all he cared about.

Until that same son had died in a freak, horse riding accident.

Her father had been as devastated as he'd been outraged, and had immediately ordered his daughter back home. That he didn't care about Arabelle's grief shouldn't have come as a shock, but after living abroad for twelve years, she'd almost forgotten the ways of her people...of her father.

She'd barely had time to grieve and process her brother's death when the arranged marriage had been forced upon her just two months after the funeral. Her father wanted a grandson, and in the bargain he got a son-in-law whose name was even more venerated than his own.

She swiped a hand over her face, fine particles of sand drifting free. The sedan she'd stolen from one of the maids or cleaning personnel had been a terrible decision. Not only was it useless on the sandy roads, its navigation system was clunky and barely useable, and its fuel was fast running out.

The decision to escape had been reckless. But when fate had all but fallen into her lap, thanks to the sandstorm, it had been an opportunity too good to refuse. She felt bad for stealing the car, but she'd find a way to recompense the owner.

She glanced into the rearview mirror again, her heart in her throat. Right now she had more serious issues to be concerned about. The line of black SUV's closing in from behind her was the same fleet of vehicles used by the highly professional security team who trailed her husband everywhere he went.

The same team who'd take her running away as a grave insult to their sheikh.

Shit. What had she been thinking? If they caught her she'd no longer be their honored sheikha. She could imagine their disgust as they mishandled her, perhaps even tortured her before bringing her back, shamed and disgraced, to their revered leader.

She shook her head. They had to capture her first.

The fuel light flashed on the dashboard in front of her. *Shit.* She was running out of options...fast.

Think, Arabelle, think!

Except there was no time for thinking, only for doing. She swung the car off the road and toward a sand dune, then drove behind it. With any luck the unsettled breeze that had continued after the sandstorm would hide any tracks in the sand.

She killed the engine and opened the window to better hear the approaching SUV's. Within minutes they roared toward her, then slowed, and her chest expanded as she held her breath for long seconds. As the vehicles continued on she exhaled roughly, left dizzy as adrenaline slowly seeped out of her.

She had no idea if going left or right at the T-intersection was the direction she needed to go, but driving the opposite way to the sheikh's security men was obviously in her best interest. She'd get as far as her fuel would allow, then she'd flag down a passing motorist and hope like hell she wasn't recognized.

She looked down at her priceless wedding gown, the bodice studded with diamonds. Her veil and diamond tiara had been thrown carelessly onto the passenger seat. She smiled. The tiara alone would be worth enough to blackmail a passing motorist into taking her out of the country.

That Mahindar had given into her one and only request for a small, western wedding, might actually pay dividends now.

She leaned forward to turn the key and fire up the engine, only to freeze at the escalating, tinny sound that sounded like a mower. Hysteria threatened. There wasn't a blade of grass out here! Nothing but sand and dunes for as far as the eye could see. Her pulse pounding in her ears, she unlocked her muscles and leaned out of the window and looked up.

Her mouth dropped open and, for a moment, she couldn't breathe. *A drone.* Of course it was. Mahindar had the highest tech at his fingertips. He'd probably had it follow her from the moment she'd raced outside and searched every car for a set of keys that might be sitting in the ignition.

It hadn't mattered at the time that the crappiest car in Rajhabi to have possibly ever entered the palace gates was the first one she'd found with keys. To her mind providence had saved her and freedom had beckoned.

Being a sheikha to one of the wealthiest sheikh's on the planet had meant nothing. She was bright enough to know she'd be little more than an exotic bird locked away in a gilded prison, whose only requirement was to breed sons for her husband.

The drone glided lower and she stared at it, numb now to the realization there *was* no escape. Not from Mahindar. He was proud to the marrow of his bones. He'd never forgive her for betraying him and his people.

Her whole body stiffened. She'd never been a quitter and wasn't about to start now. She was *not* giving up. "Fuck you, Mahindar," she snarled, flicking the bird at the drone and its cameras.

She ducked back inside the car, then leaned forward and twisted the key. *Click. Click. Click.* "What the hell?" she gritted.

"Going somewhere, my treacherous little wife?"

She jerked in her seat, then slowly cricked her neck to watch her dark-suited husband approach. But of course he'd be the one to find her. He was one of the few sheikhs' who refused to be chauffeured around and instead drove his own car. He apparently had quite the collection of them.

She gulped at his shiny, polished shoes. They were strangely hypnotizing as he strode across the swirling sand like his ancestors of old. But it mattered little that he wore western clothes with his raven black hair styled and modern. He still honored the traditions of old.

Her palms grew clammy and her heartbeat raced until she thought it might explode in her chest. This was it, then. Her prison sentence had started.

Mahindar might as well be the devil with his tight, set jaw and designer-stubble, his stony dark eyes and hard, unreadable expression. That the same man had women falling over his feet for attention was both perplexing and all too obvious. He was as handsome as he was ruthless.

But she refused to cower and show any fear. She knew how to deal with men like that...men like her egotistical father. Because though he, too, was a tyrant, he'd broken with tradition when he'd married the blonde English woman who was Arabelle's mother, and kept her as his only bride. That he'd married her against his advisors wishes left Arabelle in no doubt she'd inherited her father's stubborn streak.

But though her mother was English, it didn't make Arabelle any less of a sheikha. She had the blood of great ancestors running through her veins, too.

Her husband pulled open the driver's door, then held out his hand. Gritting her teeth, she grabbed her headdress and tiara with one hand, and took his firm grasp with the other. She refused to look at him, especially not when the shooting tingles at his touch threatened to give away her secret fascination toward him.

She quelled the reaction to instead focus on the fact he hadn't used that same hand to punish her. Though women's rights were growing in the Arab nations, disobedient women had few rights. That she'd defied her powerful sheikh husband was a whole law unto itself.

"Come," he said in his smooth, English voice with its cultured accent that made him as mysterious as the punishment he'd likely devised.

"I don't suppose I have a choice," she said in her most unshakeable, regally cool voice.

"A pity you didn't think of that earlier."

She had so much more to say, but she'd choke on her words before speaking them aloud. She was certain her punishment would be awful enough without adding to it unnecessarily.

But whatever dignity she had immediately dissolved as she stumbled, her heels sinking deep into the sand as she followed his long stride away from the sedan. His mouth thinning as he turned to her, he bent and lifted her into his arms.

She went boneless and limp—there was no longer any point in fighting—one of her arms dangling so that her priceless veil scraped along the sand. She stifled sudden hysteria. His tailored suit and shoes alone cost more than most people made in six months.

She closed her eyes, focusing on her heartbeat that thudded in her ears, her dry throat and the nauseous twist in her stomach. Anything but the powerful strength of his arms, his intoxicating amber scent and his graceful, effortless walk.

But her eyelids fluttered open soon enough, focusing on his full lips that were presently pulled tight, his high cheekbones and jet-black eyes. Even his hooked nose, which should have detracted from his good looks, somehow enhanced them. Add in six foot three of lean, corded power along with a brilliant mind, which allowed him to fluently speak six languages, and he was her worst nightmare come to life.

He was too clever, too cunning. And after her feeble attempt at escape he'd make certain she'd never have the opportunity again. That she was attracted to him even as she loathed him meant she was also fighting against herself.

Despite the heat, the sand, the grueling effort if must have taken to carry her across the soft sand, he barely drew a sweat. He could have just as easily stepped out of a bathroom from having a cool shower when he deposited her on her feet. Right next to his BMX X6, the luxury crossover SUV that was both practical and luxuriously stylish.

Meanwhile she was hot, bedraggled and exhausted. Not to mention secretly fearful of whatever punishment Mahindar had devised for her. But she refused to apologize, refused to beg for mercy. She was royalty, too.

She refused to submit to him.

He opened the front passenger door, then gestured for her to get in. Her whole body tensing, she tossed in her veil and tiara, then draped the train of her gown over a shoulder and climbed into the soft, leather interior. What else could she do? It wasn't as though she had any other options. Not anymore.

The door clunked shut behind her and she stared ahead at the endless stretch of road with misty eyes. She'd never asked for this life, she'd been born into it. While most young girls dreamed of being a real-life princess, she'd spent most of her life dreaming of a freedom that was forever just out of reach.

Her time in the UK had tantalized her with what she could have, even knowing it was an impossible dream she craved with every cell in her body.

Mahindar slid into his driver's seat and clipped on his seatbelt. His presence sucked away every scrap of oxygen, his masculine, amber scent filling her senses and his brilliant eyes stripping away her defenses. "Seatbelt," he said smoothly.

She turned away from him, but like an obedient little wife, she did as he commanded. She was nothing more than a marionette whose strings had been jerked to make her conform once again.

The line of SUV's reappeared like some dreaded mirage in the distance, Mahindar's bodyguards showing remarkable timing. Mahindar gave a satisfied smirk, then steering the car around in a smooth 180, he returned the same way Arabelle had fled.

Back to the prison that was his desert palace.

Chapter Two

Mahindar clenched the steering wheel, his pulse roaring in his ears as he glanced at his gorgeous and totally reckless young bride.

Thanks to the sandstorm the little chit could have veered off the almost non-existent road and never been found. Or someone fickle and disloyal might have found her. That she was still dressed in all her lavish wedding finery would likely have made her a target. Hell, the tiara alone was a six figure item.

That she'd put her life at risk to escape from him—a sheikh who'd been on the cover of Forbes and who had women falling over themselves for his attention—set his blood to boiling point.

How was it possible that this scrap of a woman who hated him so thoroughly had captured his attention so effortlessly? Yes, she was beautiful, but then, so had all of his past lovers. What she had was something far more elusive. Something untamed and unrefined, so different to those women who were polished to mere shells of their former selves.

Even now, with his temper barely in check, it took everything he had not to stroke her exquisite body, not to touch her many shades of natural, espresso-colored hair, with its waves that had defied a hairdresser's earlier attempts at straightening into submission.

His dick jerked at her subtle, warm cinnamon scent. That he lost control of his libido around her showed how easily he was losing grip of his iron-clad will. He took pride of being in control at all times, and if he wasn't careful his wife would weaken everything he'd worked so hard to sustain.

"Whatever you have planned for me, don't for a second imagine I will break."

He stifled a groan at her outspoken resolve. That their marriage would be a battle of wills sent waves of wild anticipation and adrenaline through him even as he surreptitiously sucked in another, deeper breath of her delicious scent. *Fuck.* A part of him might want his wife to submit to him, but another part loved even more her independence and fiery spirit.

He didn't want a biddable, well trained wife. He wanted someone intelligent and headstrong, someone with the courage to speak her mind...someone who'd eventually give those same magnificent traits to his children.

You asked for it. Now you get to deal with it.

He scraped a hand over the stubble of his jaw. As much as his traditionalist side wanted to punish her, he refused to dampen her spirit. Instead he'd prove to her that being his wife was a privilege, not a prison sentence.

Only if she continued resisting his every move would he consider disciplining her. He kept his smile on the inside. And it wouldn't be the kind of punishment she'd expect.

He sobered a little. Although her father, Sheikh Abdul, was old-school and believed in strong discipline, Arabelle hadn't been raised by him, not for a lot of years. No doubt she'd forgotten the sting of authority and had never really faced the consequences of her actions.

Mahindar's dick strained against his pants. Would his stubborn bride secretly enjoy a flogging with one of his many whips and riding crops he kept in his palace bedroom? Perhaps she'd even find pleasure in being chained to his four poster bed while he brought her close to orgasm with his hands and mouth.

Bringing her close to climax but not allowing her to have one would be the ultimate punishment for someone used to getting her own way. He exhaled roughly, his stomach contracting. Only once she was livid with passionate rage would he allow her to succumb and enjoy the best orgasm of her life.

Because he had serious doubts *any* of her past lovers had known how to satisfy her deepest, darkest needs.

His smile turned grim, warmth flooding through him and his dick nothing short of a steel pike as he imagined fulfilling her every desire. He'd start vanilla and work his way into far more complex yearnings.

That she'd been raised in a western world meant she'd probably never given a man control, even briefly, in the bedroom. She would have been too busy reveling in her freedom and ruling her own life while connecting with sensitive new age men who had no clue how to say no to her while trying to keep her happy.

A knot formed in his gut. Just how many men *had* she been with? And why did it matter? He'd been with countless women. Yet he had a feeling he'd need every bit of that experience to set his wife's passionate nature free.

It might be to his advantage that she assumed he'd married her to bind a powerful alliance with her father, Sheikh Abdul Al Hussam. She didn't need to know an alliance wasn't remotely necessary. Mahindar's affluence was legendary and he had more than enough of his own allies without her father's influence.

She needed to know even less that her father had secured this union thanks to the war threatening at his borders. Arabelle had unknowingly and unwittingly saved her people thanks to Mahindar's powerful and influential friends.

In all honesty, Sheikh Abdul al Hussam was nothing more than a burr in Mahindar's side, a nuisance he could do without.

His daughter, though, was another thing entirely.

Mahindar glanced at her again, admiring her smooth brow, passionate, full lips and the delicate length of her nose she'd inherited from her western mother. His eyes narrowed as he noted the elegant line of her throat, where her pulse beat furiously.

Was she that frightened of him? He might have a fierce reputation, but he wasn't unfair. He understood much of what his gorgeous bride railed against. Life for many Middle East women wasn't easy. But it didn't have to be a battleground, either. If she allowed him in, her life could be the fairytale most girls dreamed about.

That she wouldn't just surrender to any man kept his dick hard and his interest absolute. It would take a strong, powerful and yet restrained touch to break down her resistance. And he was just the man to do it.

She glowered at him, her striking blue-green eyes—another trait handed down to her from her gorgeous mother—holding his. "What is it you intend to do with me?"

He stifled a groan. If his dick was a steel pike earlier, it was a concrete pillar now. Just imagining all the sex positions he'd introduce to her kept his seed boiling like a pressure cooker in his nuts. He had no reason to believe she was a virgin. But he also doubted her lovers had shown her much in the way of passion and technique.

Yet her mind and her body were made for loving.

"Well?" she demanded, dissolving all his fantasies into mist.

"What do *you* think I should do with you?" he asked mildly, though there was nothing mild in the way he reacted to her.

She lifted her chin. "I think you should do the right thing and release me."

His whole body tensed. If she'd read his thoughts she'd know *right* wasn't in his best interests and freeing her wouldn't happen in a million years. "Really?" he drawled.

She nodded, apparently reading his neutral tone as an opportunity. "Yes! You could put me in your helicopter and never have to see me again. We can even live as man and wife on separate continents for a few months to appease our people, and when the time is right, we'll sign the divorce papers."

"In Rajhabi, a marriage is for life. If you'd taken any interest at all in our nation you would have known this."

While other women would have been deflated at his comment, she seemed even more determined to a battle of wills. "As a sheikh highly respected by your people and your peers, you can change those old-fashioned rulings. We're in the twenty-first century, not—"

"Those old fashioned rulings are from generations of time-honored and valued traditions. In an ever-changing world, that one constant keeps my people happy. Changing them now would start nothing less than a revolt."

"Maybe from your men," she muttered derisively.

"More so from the women," he corrected. "They love tradition and take great pride in ensuring it's passed on to their children."

The palace came into sight then, its huge white walls and domed spires shimmering under the setting sun. Fierce joy moved through him. He was proud of his homeland, his people and his culture, and though he agreed that some traditions could be modernized, he wasn't about to rush into it. His people were his voice and he acted on their behalf.

He glanced at his wife again. He wanted to believe she'd do the right thing by their people, too. But was she too self-centered to have their best interests at heart? Her running away had proven how little she cared about anyone but herself. His nation had never been better off, both economically and politically. War was a distant memory along with poverty, and he intended to keep it that way.

Keeping his tone mild, he said, "You're so determined to run from our marriage before giving it a chance. It seems to me you're more scared of change than any number of my people."

She looked out the side window then, as though caught out by the truth. "I've had more time in the western world than I have here. I rejoiced in my freedom and never thought I'd have to return and marry royalty."

"What you're objecting to is almost every other woman's fantasy."

She sniffed. "Then I guess I'm not like every other woman."

He couldn't have agreed more.

Chapter Three

Arabelle shivered as her husband drove between the huge stone pillars, where metal gates opened automatically. She'd only managed to escape in the first place thanks to a late wedding guest who'd entered the gates. As they'd swung open she'd shot through, leaving the solitary guard behind to raise the alarm.

Mahindar parked in front of the palace's grand entrance, where marble stairs marched up to engraved double doors. Either side of the steps, large palm trees swayed and clumps of ornamental grasses made everything look plush. Pools of water with fountains jetted water, as though mocking the parched desert outside the walls.

He didn't appear to take any notice of his wealth. He looked stern and forbidding as he unfolded his long length from the driver's seat and walked around the SUV to open her passenger door.

"Come," he said. "There is much I need to do before our honeymoon."

"Honeymoon?" she repeated numbly, before accepting his hand and stepping out of the SUV. She looked back at her tiara and headdress. "Oh, I should probably—"

"Leave them," he said without a trace of emotion. "My men will see to their return."

As he shut the door behind her, a man in a white thobe and keffiyeh headdress took the driver's seat and drove the SUV to the back of the palace, to where she guessed there was a big garage for all of Mahindar's fancy cars.

Mahindar managed a half-smile that showcased gorgeous white teeth and twin dimples. "And yes, *honeymoon.* Right now we're barely more than strangers. A honeymoon is the perfect opportunity to get to know one another."

She cleared her throat and pulled her hand free. "To be honest I wasn't sure how important this marriage was to you. I mean, you must have unlimited women willing to be your bride, women who'd lick your toes if you asked them." She gazed up at him. "Why did my dad sign a contract for you to marry me? Was it money?"

His jaw tightened, a muscle jerking into life in one cheek. "I didn't want or ask for a dowry. It is no secret Rajhabi's economy is exceptional and growing."

"So what *is* it you want?" she asked, her eyes narrowing at him. "A dozen sons? I'm sure there are also plenty of fertile women—"

"I'm hoping for daughters, too," he interjected drily, obviously no longer interested in hearing about every other, willing woman available to him.

She blinked, gauging his sincerity. "Would you value your daughters as much as you would your sons?"

"Of course." He cocked his head to the side. "Did your father not regard you as highly as he did your brother?"

"If you mean would he have mourned me as deeply as he did my brother, then no. His son was his pride and joy, the man who'd one day take over his rule." She lifted her chin, barely withholding her pain. "I loved my brother, too. But I'd like to believe even he saw the unfairness of my father's treatment. I'd also like to believe he'd understand why I ran away from this marriage to you."

Mahindar stayed silent as he took the crook of her arm and led her past the misty fountains and rustling palm trees, then up the marble stairs. She looked around. Already the sand had been cleared away, with only a few particles daring to roll along the long, wide steps.

His staff were efficient, the palace a place of beauty in such an unforgiving desert landscape. Not that this was his only residence. He kept a smaller palace in the city, but rumor had it he much preferred the solitary existence of his desert home.

They stepped inside the palace, where chandeliers and downlights automatically brightened the gloom and pushed back the shadows of an approaching nightfall. Though she'd already seen inside she couldn't help but be awed all over again. Huge gold frames showcased ancient needlework and priceless oil paintings on the stone walls, while portraits of his ancestors were hung at wide-spaced intervals along a corridor where three cars could have easily passed through.

She shuddered at the images of Mahindar's descendants. The Al Qantisi men were undeniably charismatic and fierce, the women beautiful and haughty. That those same genetics and traits had clearly been passed onto Mahindar left her feeling more than a little weak at the knees.

Who was she to imagine she'd outwit possibly the greatest sheikh in history? A man who'd taken a rundown, war-ridden nation and made it one of the mightiest nations on Earth? There were only three other sheikhs who rivaled him. That all three had been at her and Mahindar's wedding and were obviously great friends made everything seem even more insurmountable.

Her husband had powerful friends. She had no one but herself.

Any self-pity fled as they came to the last two paintings on the wall, which showcased his parents. Both had been dead for almost a decade after being killed in a mortar attack in a long ago war.

She'd heard the stories. He'd been nineteen when they had died, and far too young to take over the responsibility of running a country. Yet here he was a decade later and not quite thirty years old ruling Rajhabi with a skill of someone three times his age. That he'd turned his reign into something prosperous and peaceful was a credit to him.

Not that he'd done it without his share of ruthlessness. To achieve greatness he hadn't been shy in doing what needed to be done, including marrying her.

She sighed. Not that her father's reign had been nearly as stellar. He'd acquired many enemies along the way to making his nation rich. Many of those same enemies now threatened his region's borders. A sour taste filled her mouth. She'd bet that unrest had settled quite a lot though since his daughter's marriage to Mahindar.

Well played, Dad. Well played.

"You probably heard about my parents deaths," he said in an undertone, pausing between the paintings for a moment as though showing his respect.

"I did. Your nation was already in turmoil. But their death created a whole lot more unrest."

He nodded. "It took great patience and perseverance to earn back my peoples trust and respect."

She arched a brow. "Earn it back? You were only nineteen. You were as innocent as those who were victims of the war."

"At the time I felt as bloodied and guilty as anyone else in the violence that killed so many. I'll do everything in my power to never endure another war again. At least, not in my lifetime." He drew her away from the portraits and even managed a smile. "I'm just glad you know a little of my nation's history."

"Even when I was away I wasn't completely immune to the goings on that happened over here. I was ten when your parents were murdered, and I still recall it vividly."

"So young," he murmured with a frown. "That I was taking on leadership of Rajhabi while you were probably still playing with dolls—"

"Hardly playing with dolls," she interjected. "I had to grow up fast, too. I'd had no choice. My English skills were second-rate at best, and I'd had to juggle extra classes just to catch up. Which meant my social life was almost non-existent."

He guided her up some curved, majestic stairs to the next level. "Was it?" he mused aloud. "From all accounts you formed strong friendships with many women and men."

She glanced up at his dark tone. "I formed friendships...eventually," she conceded. "Men seemed rather enamored with my looks and accent. And those women who didn't judge my appearance were really quite nice."

At the top of the landing he drew her left. There was no hallway, just a big door that he pushed open to reveal a huge master bedroom suite, more spacious than most people's entire homes. He bent and picked her up, then stepped inside. "I've been waiting to carry you across the threshold from the moment I slid the ring on your finger and kissed your luscious lips."

She did her best to ignore her body's traitorous reaction to being in his strong arms once again. Instead she looked down at the simple wedding ring, realizing how right it felt on her finger. As for the kiss that sealed their marriage...

She'd been shocked by the electric jolt of awareness between them. That same kiss had burned its way through her body, and sent her running scared even before she'd actually found a way to escape.

He placed her back on her feet, then cupped her face. Tracing her lips with his thumb, he murmured, "I have a few things I need to clear. But I'm sure you'll want to get out of your gown and take a shower, wash off all that sand before we travel."

A frisson of electricity zinged through her lips and straight to her core. She fought to stay lucid, logical. "You're leaving me?"

He smirked. "For the moment. But don't go getting any ideas. There is no escape for you this time. I have my security team stationed around the palace at every access point. And I believe you're too smart to try a second time." He leaned close, his lips claiming hers for a handful of heated seconds. Long enough for her heart to race and tingles to cascade down her spine to her toes. He pulled back and added softly, "We both know the consequences of such an action would be...dire."

Chapter Four

Arabelle ran a hand down the soft fabric of the fluttery aqua, knee length dress that was clearly haute couture. Her husband had a good eye for women's measurements. Not just for the dress but her silky thong and bra, too. Even her heeled shoes were a perfect fit.

That he'd also sent a hairdresser and nail technician to their bedroom after she'd showered was enough for her to digest. Luckily they'd been quick and efficient. While one woman had upswept her hair into a fancy knot with pearl side-combs, the other one had moisturized her hands and feet, filed her nails and painted them a cherry red.

The moment Mahindar had returned, his staff had quietly withdrew. If his eyes weren't already dark enough, they'd darkened further on seeing her. But he'd simply taken her hand and led her through the palace before they took some stairs onto the roof.

The cool, velvet night air brushing her skin, he'd bundled her into his helicopter, checked her headset before he took the pilot's seat. She noted some pieces of luggage in the back but was soon distracted by the dizzying liftoff.

It took perhaps a minute to leave the lights of the palace behind, but she was amazed at how quickly lights again twinkled into existence as they flew close to the outskirts of Ninuk, his nation's biggest city.

Landing on a helipad at his private airstrip, he escorted her out of the helicopter to a luxury Gulfstream jet which awaited them on the tarmac. Everything happened so fast her head was spinning even before the jet idled down the runway then surged into a take-off that soon had them gliding up into the sky.

It was surreal sitting next to her husband in one of the jet's soft, cream leather seats, with air hostesses taking care of their every need and offering a vast menu along with refreshments.

Though she declined any suggestions, Mahindar ordered the baklava and champagne.

"It's a bit early in the morning for alcohol, isn't it?" she asked after one of the stunning air hostesses sashayed through the front door to fetch his request.

He smiled. "We've yet to sleep. It's been a long day and an even longer night, and you look like you could use a drink to help you relax."

He also appeared to delight in feeding her the honey-sweet, many-layered filo pastry filled with chopped nuts. But though her stomach at first cramped in rejection at the thought of food, after she nibbled at one corner, she could no longer say no to her favorite treat of all time. *Had he known that?*

With his blunt-ended fingertips touching her lips and sending warm sparks through her body, along with the bubbly drink she swallowed automatically, she was soon not just relaxing; she was becoming warm and fuzzy inside.

Even the dawn light, which at first had been nothing more than a suggestion outside the windows, began to brighten the sky and finally glisten on the blue waters of the Mediterranean Sea below them in invitation.

Mahindar's dark gaze settled on her. "We'll be landing in ten minutes."

His comment evaporated her feel-good vibes, reminding her of why she was really here. She sent him a strained smile, all the while wishing she was home in the UK. Because that *was* her home now, no matter how much her husband made her heart race when he was near. That being married to Mahindar made her a sheikha to a region she knew so little about only made her more homesick.

She nodded, but didn't ask about his choice of honeymoon. It wasn't like he'd given her any preference. He'd no doubt take her to some exotic, over-the-top resort where people flaunted their wealth and tried to outdo one another.

Instead they landed on a tiny island's airstrip, where a chauffeur waited on the tarmac in an open-topped Jeep. It was kind of fun to sit in the back next to Mahindar, his big hand engulfing hers while the sea air whipped at her fancy hairdo and the rising sun showcased breathtaking views of the Mediterranean ocean, seagulls wheeling above their jeep and the glittering, white capped waves.

They passed a village where children kicked around a ball while others practiced throwing their fishing nets, dogs running around madly barking. Some of the children ran beside the Jeep, calling out and waving, and Mahindar waved back, his smile wide and his eyes flashing amusement.

A pang filled her chest. What would he be like with his own children, *their* children? Would he be a loving father or a strict tyrant like her dad had been? That her mother still loved him, despite his flaws, made Arabelle more determined than ever not to fall for a man who didn't show his love in return.

A house came into view, then, and her introspection faded as she sat forward to better see what appeared to be their honeymoon destination. The red-cedar home sat high on stilts next to the edge of a sandy embankment. And though the home appeared quaint, in other ways it was modern, too, with its many tinted windows taking advantage of the ocean views.

She blinked. She'd expected some huge mansion with servants scurrying around. Instead he'd chosen something intimate and inviting. Something personal and tasteful.

"Not what you were expecting?" he asked shrewdly.

"It's not," she conceded softly. Then added, "It's perfect."

He smiled. "I thought you might enjoy some alone time, away from everyone including the paparazzi."

She nodded. "I'm not up to dealing with any of that yet."

"You had much freedom in the UK, didn't you?"

"I did. I was anonymous. Not even my closest friends knew I was a sheikha." At least, not until she was taken away from her life in the UK. She sighed. "It was wonderful."

He frowned a little, as though caught unawares by her comment. "Most women I know adore the limelight."

Just how many women had he known? Bad enough he kept a harem, as was the custom, but to enjoy foreign women as well had her stomach ball into knots. "I suppose most women want everyone to know they're with you," she said in what she hoped was a vaguely dismissive voice.

"And yet my own wife will do anything to get away from me."

She didn't say anything to that. Instead she looked away as the driver parked the jeep at the roadside entrance to the house.

Mahindar climbed out and proffered her a hand. She accepted, managing a smile as they stepped across a ramp that bridged a sandy embankment and its drop-off to the beach below, straight to the back door. Their driver took their luggage from the back of the jeep and followed them across as Mahindar keyed in a security code.

The door swung open, revealing bright rugs on hardwood floors that smelled of beeswax. A cream-brick fireplace was a feature in the living room, while the open plan dining room revealing a warm oak table and the kitchen showcased a stone island countertop and stainless steel appliances.

The driver placed their luggage into what must be their bedroom, and Mahindar spoke briefly to the man before the servant nodded deferentially and withdrew.

"What do you think?" Mahindar asked as she looked out the huge windows at the front of the house. A high deck beckoned to the L-shaped flight of steps outside, which led to a private beach below.

"The views are spectacular," she conceded.

He stepped behind her. "They are," he murmured, giving her the impression he was talking about a far different view than the one she was looking at. He wrapped his arms around her waist from behind. "You must be exhausted after being awake all night."

She stiffened, hating that he wanted sex to impregnate her even as her body threatened to melt into his powerful embrace. "You were awake, too," she said hoarsely.

"Mm. But then I'm used to little sleep."

She swallowed back spiteful words. Who needed sleep when he had so many women at his beck and call? He was spoilt for choice in that regard. And yet here he was stuck with his little churlish wife, whose only claim to fame was a diluted bloodline that made her royalty.

He bent and kissed behind her ear, his warm breath somehow stroking her senses and sending skittering goosebumps down her spine. "I think a shower might be in order," he murmured huskily, "followed by bed."

Her mouth dried and her muscles locked and he sighed as he dropped his arms from around her waist, then captured one of her hands with his own. "Come."

There was no point in trying to resist. Her strength was puny compared to his and she didn't want to find out if he'd force his disobedient wife into the shower if she dug in her heels. She'd somehow avoided punishment so far and she wanted to keep it that way.

She followed him into the bedroom, her heels sinking into plush carpet and her vision filling with the four-poster bed, where he would soon lay her out and claim her as his own. Her heart pumping and throat thick, she stepped onto big white tiles inside the en suite, where double shower heads and gleaming taps beckoned.

"Allow me," he said throatily, bending to clasp the hem of her dress and draw it up and over her head. She lifted her arms obediently, her body caught between stiff rejection and an odd, buzzing arousal as he tossed the dress aside and exhaled appreciatively. "Beautiful."

She swallowed hard at his comment. But though the cream bra and thong did indeed look great on her warm complexion with her naturally slender body, she was all too aware he'd dated supermodels and slept with women in his harem whose looks were their highest prerequisite.

She lifted her chin. "You don't need to charm me into bed. Let's just get this over with."

Chapter Five

If Mahindar hadn't been so damn hard with desire he might have laughed at his wife's shocking suggestion. Get it over with? He smirked. He'd soon change her mind. She'd be gasping and groaning beneath him. But not before he worked her into pre-orgasmic bliss in the shower.

He took out her pearl side combs and released her hair, running his fingers through her glorious mane. The strands were so soft and thick and inviting, and framed her gorgeous face to perfection.

He bent and took his time removing her heeled shoes. Her ankles were so slender and her feet so small and delicate. Yet nothing about his wife was meek. She was fiery and stubborn, and so unlike the women of his region he wondered if his people must think him mad to marry her.

Then he drew down her thong and all thoughts dissolved like mist on the desert dunes. *Exquisite.* He drew apart her folds and gently exhaled on the pearl between her folds. Her breath hissed and his pulse thudded in his ears. *Oh, yes.* He'd enjoy every second of her yielding to him.

He flicked her sensitized clit and it bloomed from his touch, swelling and flushing. His dick responded in kind, hardening to the point of pain. As much as he wanted to lick and suck her pussy, to graze her with his teeth and kiss away the sting, his willpower wasn't invincible.

He needed to be inside her before he exploded.

He straightened and her head tipped back, her beautiful eyes holding his as he brushed his hands along her back and unclipped her bra. When her breasts spilled free his groan spilled free, too. She wasn't small everywhere. He bent and licked one of her pink nipples and it sprang into a hard, tempting nub.

He closed his eyes, doing whatever was necessary to dim his senses and rein in his urgent desire. A pity he was saturated by her heady scent of warm cinnamon that mingled with her arousal. Even her quickening breaths and the beat of her frantic pulse at the base of her throat drew him in.

He clamped his lips together and threw her bra aside. Then opening the shower screen door, he drew her with him into the large cubicle before he pulled the lever, releasing jets of warm, pulsing water from the double showerheads.

The water streamed over them and his chest tightened at the sight of his wet goddess, her lips parting and her cheeks flushed. He bent and took possession of her mouth. When she drew in a sharp breath, then began to kiss him back, Mahindar groaned into her mouth and snagged her hair in one fisted hand.

He wanted so badly to dominate, to take and take and take. Though virgins were highly prized and a part of him wished he was her first, another part was glad she wasn't. Not when his urgent needs might otherwise scare her away for good. He'd wipe all her lovers from her memory and make her crave him like an addict until no other drug sufficed.

His hold tightened and she bent her head back, lessening the pressure on her scalp and exposing her throat. He kissed his way down the slender column, loving her wet, silken warmth, her fluttering pulse.

His little wife was succumbing fast.

That he wanted to mark her and let the world know she was his made his cock steely-hard. He sucked on her neck until her unsteady moan reminded him to release her before he bruised her skin too badly.

He lifted his head and looked down into her dazed, blue-green eyes, where water droplets beaded her long, dark lashes. The mark already forming on her throat made his pulse tattoo loudly in his ears. "You're mine," he said hoarsely. "You'll always be mine."

Shutting off the water pressure, he bent and lifted her into his arms. Both of them dripping wet, he carried her out of the bathroom and across the carpeted floor of the bedroom, then laid her at the end of the bed.

It was time to claim his wife.

Chapter Six

Arabelle had never had such an out-of-body experience. She was physically engaged and aroused, but her mind was barely along for the ride. Like someone observing a dream as it unfolded.

Making love to Mahindar might as well be happening to someone else.

What would her husband say if she revealed the truth? Then told him she'd never been with anyone else? Not that she'd deliberately saved her virginity, she'd just never found a man worthy of giving it to.

She swallowed hard. That her husband was so big all over and his desire so urgent meant he wasn't going to be gentle. Despite his skilled foreplay her body was now wound so tight she feared his possession of her and how much it would hurt. She shivered. If he was possessive of her now, she could only imagine his triumph at discovering she was a virgin.

He leaned over her, his long golden body following her onto the bed and his hard cock grazing her inner thigh. She closed her eyes. She'd get through this. It was nothing more than a marital obstacle. He'd take her once or twice and his duty would be done and he'd return to his harem.

Then she'd be free...as free as one could get once she was locked in his desert palace. That something burned inside her chest while thinking about his indiscretions behind her back wasn't worth dwelling upon.

She'd do her duty and become impregnated. She'd even try to be a dutiful wife and queen to his people.

Then his mouth covered hers and she squeezed her eyes closed as sensation threatened to engage her mind to her body. His mouth might at times be hard but right then his lips were soft and coaxing, warm and inviting.

He was an amazing kisser, his experience in the bedroom all too apparent.

"Open your eyes, *habibi*."

Her eyes flew apart at his endearment. She stared into his brilliant dark eyes. *My love* wasn't a word to be said lightly. She was so occupied with the thought she barely noticed when he one-handed his shaft to guide it to her core.

Yet in one thrust he shut down her mind while her whole world tore apart and a distant, pained cry—her own—shattered the strained silence.

She absently noted his wide-eyed disbelief, his tightly-strung body and his cock that was wedged so tight and deep inside her she wondered if he'd ever dislodge it from her.

"Stay with me, *habibi*," he said thickly, and though his long black lashes showcased his passionate intensity that was as quickly also turning into something triumphant and possessive, she was shielded from any further emotions.

She was far, far away. Somewhere pain didn't touch her and dreams of another life still sparkled within reach.

"Arabelle, look at me," he commanded harshly, his gaze narrowing.

She did as he asked, but she wasn't there with him, not really.

Even when he began moving inside her, and the pain drifted into a faint ache as her body unwittingly responded, she kept inside her head. Then he kissed her again, an almost desperate merging of lips that struck a chord deep inside her.

He was getting to her! Somehow he was untangling the knots around her heart as skillfully as some renowned cardiologist.

"That's it," he said thickly, his voice edged with urgent passion. "Don't fight me. Not now...not in this."

She closed her eyes. How could she possibly fight? He was a master at making love and she was an inexperienced virgin. Already the heat inside her body was encompassing her mind until she was glowing and incandescent with need.

"Perfect," he groaned. *"You're* perfect."

It was his words that ultimately set her off. She was a firecracker set alight then exploding, the orgasm hitting her hard and fast. She gasped then cried out as she flew high, her inner muscles contracting and setting Mahindar off, too.

He groaned long and loud, his head falling back and a muscle in his jaw jumping into life as his seed rushed out, filling her with even more warmth.

Her chest heaving as she caught her breath, she gazed up at her magnificent husband, resisting an urge to run her hands through his thick, raven hair and get lost in his now warm, liquid black eyes.

He adjusted his position a little so that he his strong forearms rested on the mattress either side of her to stop his body from crushing her.

She should have been on top of the world, delighted they were so compatible in bed. Instead she was infuriated. He wasn't supposed to touch her emotionally. It was her one safe place.

They might be married but she was more than just his wife, and she refused to lose that one part of herself to him. So why did emptiness assail her the moment he disconnected from her?

He cupped her chin and raised her gaze to his. His expression inscrutable, he asked, "Why didn't you tell me you were a virgin?"

"Would it really have mattered?" Damn it, her voice quivered like his answer *did* matter to her.

"You know it would," he said with a distinct edge in his voice, like he couldn't believe she'd question it. "I would have been gentler, more considerate." He exhaled, then disconnected gently before pushing off the bed to stand looking down at her. "What you gave me is priceless, a gift."

She clapped her legs together and tried not to feel exposed and awkward under his astute gaze. But though she might be physically naked, it was her stripped mental state that alarmed her. "I'm glad I was able to offer you something in this marriage," she said hoarsely.

He bent a little and proffered her a hand, and after a split second hesitation, she accepted his grasp. He pulled her to her feet, and she resisted rubbing at the goose-bumps on her arms at how tall and powerful he was and how diminutive she was next to him. Her head barely reached his shoulders!

She couldn't help but glance at his powerful nakedness. She swallowed hard. His ability to have sex with her again so soon was frighteningly obvious and all too tempting. But though a reckless part of her wanted him again, another part of her wanted to coldly dismiss any advances.

If only his masculinity wasn't so damn pronounced! That he'd fit inside her seemed impossible now. Like a triangle slotting into a square.

His dark eyes held hers. But if he noted her flushed face and fluttery pulse he didn't let on. Instead he said softly, "Don't ever imagine you're anything less than someone else. Not ever, my little bride. Your passion and your strength of mind mean everything to me."

She nodded. What could she even say to that? Most sheikhs expected docile, obedient wives and lovers. But then Mahindar wasn't an average sheikh. He was brilliant and startlingly popular with his people, a man who was surrounded by his adoring fans one moment, and reclusive and hiding away the next.

"Come," he said gently, the back of his hand running down the side of her face. "Let's get some sleep. You'll have plenty of time to dissect me and our marriage once you're awake again."

Her face heated. *Oh, crap.* She'd been *that* obvious?

He chuckled as he pulled down the covers and she climbed into bed. When he followed her and his big, warm body tucked her close, she was a little surprised to realize she felt safe for the first time in forever.

Wriggling closer and only vaguely aware of his hissed breath, she closed her eyes and allowed the darkness to take her away.

Chapter Seven

Arabelle laughed with her friends as they entered the bar and grill. They were all in the mood to celebrate; after all, it wasn't every day the pressure of final exams was behind them.

They were now ready to take on the editing world. That Arabelle had barely strung an English sentence together on arrival in the UK let alone become gifted in the written word still made her smile.

"My treat," Scott announced after pulling his wallet out of his designer jacket pocket with a flourish. As everyone cheered in agreement, he added gleefully, his eyes catching hold of Arabelle's, "But I get to choose the drinks!"

"Whatever," Kiki said enthusiastically, her wild auburn curls bouncing against her shoulders, "if you're buying we're drinking!"

Arabelle smiled at her roommate's gusto. But then Kiki never did anything by halves and sometimes it reminded Arabelle that she, too, was no longer constrained by the place of her birth.

She accepted her shot glass of tequila, then drank it down with the rest of her friends. Alcohol wasn't something she indulged in often and by the fourth shot she was a little woozy and warm, and wonderfully relaxed. Not even Scott's constant gaze on her could detract from her night.

Kiki giggled and whispered in her ear, "Scott is hot for you. You know he's a great catch. Rich, good looking, charming. If you want to have a little fun you could do a whole lot worse than him."

The band in the corner of the room started up, playing eighties rock and roll that blared from the speakers while the sultry, husky tones of the singer sounded remarkably like Joan Jett.

Scott proffered Arabelle his hand. "Dance with me?"

Arabelle accepted. What could one dance hurt? "Only if you promise not to step on my toes."

"I can't promise you that with a straight face," he said with a grin as he led her toward the dance floor. "But don't worry, I won't let anything bad happen to you."

Everything abruptly jarred to a stop—the music, the laughter, the easy camaraderie—as everyone craned their necks to see the men in their Middle Eastern robes and headdresses march through the front door into the bar and grill.

Arabelle's eyes clashed with the man at the front, her father, the sheikh of Lumana. His glittering, dark eyes were filled with aversion at seeing her in such close proximity to a man. That she wore a short, glittery gown, high heels and ruby lipstick no doubt heightened his distaste. "Arabelle, you're to come home now."

She gaped. "I have job offers—"

"You *will* obey me in this."

Another man in his thobe stepped close, one Arabelle vaguely recalled. Her father's closest advisor, Yaqub. He cleared his throat. "Your family needs you now, Sheikha Arabelle."

"Sheikha?" Scott asked, his voice high-pitched and his eyes bugging out of his head.

"I don't believe it," Kiki said weakly.

Arabelle crossed her arms. She couldn't worry about her friends, not yet. Bad enough that her father had royally fucked her over and her friends would never look at her the same way again. Nor would they trust her after she'd pretended to have a normal upbringing like everyone else. "Why on earth would my family want me home? I talk to my mother regularly and I know my brother—"

"Your brother is dead," her father interjected harshly, grief flashing briefly in his eyes. "If we leave now we'll make it to his funeral."

The whole room did a slow spin as Arabelle shook her head. "His funeral," she croaked wretchedly. "I don't believe it."

Her father's advisor stepped close and drew her upright. His mouth curling with distaste at her minimalist western wear, he informed coolly, "The great sheikh doesn't lie. Your brother had a bad accident and never recovered."

She had no strength to argue or resist. Even her friends simply gaped after her as she was led out of the bar and grill and placed into the back of a sleek limousine beside the advisor, her father climbing in after her so that there was no escape.

She was left with nothing but bitter disbelief that her brother—one she barely knew—had died, and the disillusioned impression that she would have no choice now but to undertake any responsibilities he'd left behind.

Chapter Eight

Arabelle's lashes fluttered apart and Mahindar's face swam into view beside her, his sharp eyes assessing in the bright, sunlit room.

"Sleep well?" he asked smoothly, as though nothing ever dared touch him in his slumber.

She pushed a hand over her face and managed an awkward smile. Going by the dull light filtering inside it was early morning. They'd slept away most of the day and all night! "Like a baby."

"You did," he agreed, pushing a strand of her hair behind her ear. "I woke a few hours ago and watched you sleep."

Her face heated. "How...tedious."

"On the contrary, it was...fascinating. Do you always mumble and cry out when you're sleeping like a baby?"

She blinked, her mouth suddenly dry. "W-what did I say?"

His mouth curved into a half-smile. "From the bits and pieces I could understand, you didn't want to go home and leave your life in England."

Her chest tightened. Just how much had she babbled out loud? *Bloody hell.* As if marrying him against her will and having him take her virginity wasn't bad enough. She wouldn't bare her soul to him, too!

Bending his arm, he propped his head on a hand and asked idly, "Was there a special someone you were forced to leave behind?"

"N-no!" she refused hotly. But at his satisfied smirk she realized she shouldn't be telling him everything. He already had anyone and everything he wanted in his life, like they were little more than disposable toys. It would be nothing short of joyful and perhaps a little shameless to deny him her heart and pretend she'd given it to someone else.

She sighed, then pretended to look contrite. "You're right, there *was* someone else."

His eyes darkened a little and tension emanated from him. "And you still have feelings for this man?"

She squeezed her eyes closed to hide any signs of laughter. "Do you really think my feelings are so weak that marrying a stranger will change them?"

Mahindar rolled so that he was on top of her.

She jerked as his big, long body weighted her down. *Holy smokes.* His cock was already insistently pressing against her most intimate place, her body ready to arch toward his as if she were an animal in heat. Her eyes popped open to his dark gaze that ensnared hers. With his intense expression reading her every little nuance and his big body robbing her of all breath, she was already regretting her lies.

"Then let's begin the process of making you forget him until I'm the only man you think about."

"You can't want sex again so soon?" she squeaked.

He chuckled darkly. "You really are an innocent, aren't you?" he murmured. "Do you really believe having sex once with you in a night is enough?" He bent low and kissed her ear, then suckled the lobe into his mouth so that her nerve endings sent shockwaves of pleasure straight to her core. His hot breath curled her toes as he added huskily. "I'm going to fuck you until your brain is fogged and your body is exhausted, and you have no memory of anything or anyone."

He was too damn sure, too confident! And he'd probably never known the sting of rejection his entire life. She couldn't allow him to think she'd fallen for him like every other woman in his life. "You can't force me to forget. He is all I've been thinking about since leaving England."

Mahindar's face darkened. "While you're with me no other man will enter your thoughts."

"And how do you propose to do that?" she said in a quivery voice.

He one-handed his shaft and guided it between her legs. "Allow me to show you, my sweet wife."

Chapter Nine

Mahindar stared broodingly through the huge window and out to sea, the cup of coffee in his hand as yet untouched. He'd never met a woman who didn't want him, and had certainly never met one who pined for another man.

His gut clenched and he scowled. Arabelle had come undone beneath him, her glazed eyes and panting breaths revealing her loss of control. When she'd soon after looked away, he'd kissed his way down her body, starting at her lovely breasts and ending at her saturated pussy. It hadn't taken much to set her off again and with the taste of her still in his mouth he'd kissed her and possessed her all over again.

It'd taken her three orgasms before she'd fallen into another deep slumber. And it had taken everything he'd had not to tuck her close and sleep with her. But though his body wanted to succumb his mind rebelled at the idea. He sighed. He'd always liked a challenge but proving to his wife she desired no one but him was grinding his nerves to a nub.

As if her running away just hours after their vows wasn't shitty enough. Admitting she had feelings for another man pushed every boundary he had and then some.

He lifted his cup and took a sip of the bitter coffee—just how he liked it—then grimaced at the cold contents. Striding back into the kitchen, he put his cup onto the sink and headed to the door that would take him to the beach.

Though this ocean was famed for its undercurrents and rips and was far too dangerous for most swimmers, he was confident in his ability and needed the physical exertion to dim his bleak thoughts.

He peeled open the glass door and stepped naked outside, where the mid-morning sun heated his skin and the briny scent of the ocean filled his nostrils. Having his own private beach was one of the perks of his quaint holiday home. No one would disturb him or his disloyal young bride unless he required something.

Descending the stairs, he ran across the sand that squelched underfoot, the shock of cool water then an invigorating rush as he ran into it, then dived through the first wave and came up on the other side.

He continued swimming, stroking through the salty water and diving through each wave until his muscles were aching and he was far enough out that his house was matchbox size and the shore looked far away.

He trod water for a few minutes, his thoughts still preoccupied by the woman sleeping in his bed. The woman who tormented him simply by not returning his affection. But then she wasn't to know that he'd kept track of her over the last year, ever since he'd considered a bride and knew as a sheikha she'd fit perfectly in with his plans.

She'd be horrified if she learned the truth, and to know he'd even traveled to England and watched her from afar at least half-a-dozen times. And that even though he'd known after the first trip he wanted her as his future wife, the next five trips had simply been an obsession to see her again.

He smiled grimly, then surged back to shore with swift, clean strokes that cut through the salty water. The physical exertion was exactly what he needed to clear his head. His lifestyle had been getting stale of late, and his bride was just the challenge he needed to keep things interesting.

In the end it mattered little what secret desires she carried inside, because she'd have a change of heart sooner rather than later. And he'd do whatever had to be done to see to it.

Chapter Ten

Arabelle woke with a start, aware right away she was alone. The absence of Mahindar's overwhelming presence made the bedroom—the entire house—strangely empty.

That she'd sensed him gone didn't mean anything. Just because they'd had mind-blowing sex didn't make them close, certainly not soulmates. They weren't even yet friends. She snorted. They probably wouldn't ever be more than married fuck buddies. She was nothing more than a broodmare to Mahindar, a woman whose bloodline meant she was perfect for the role of bearing his children.

Moving out of the deep, luxurious bed, she padded to the walk-in-closet, where Mahindar's suits, casual clothes and shoes lined one side, while every feminine garment and fashion accessories lined the other.

Designer gowns, premium casual wear and underwear, sleepwear, shoes, sandals, boots and everything in-between. That someone had unpacked their luggage sometime after their arrival here didn't sit well with her. She valued her privacy and enjoyed her independence, even if it was something as simple as hanging up her clothes.

She sighed. This was her life now. Privacy was a thing of the past along with having to do menial tasks. From now on she should expect nothing but the best as Mahindar's wife, Sheikha of Rajhabi.

She retrieved a gossamer thin, white nightgown and slid it over her nakedness, aware that it revealed as much as it covered her body. Not that it mattered. Her husband knew her intimately now, knew every inch of her. And he would take his pleasure from her no matter what clothes she wore.

Not even a burqa would keep her safe from his virility now.

She padded out of the bedroom and toward the glass doors that were slightly ajar to the deck outside, where the salty ocean breeze filtered through the house and the sun was high in the sky.

Not that she blamed Mahindar for his virility. She hadn't exactly been prim and proper between the sheets with him, either. She'd been wanton and had reveled in everything he'd shown her, her body betraying her as one orgasm after another had rolled through her.

That she'd given every impression she enjoyed being his wife was undeniable now. But though she'd physically surrendered to him, she'd fight him mentally every step of the way. She huffed out a sardonic breath. With any luck he'd grow sick of her willfulness and send her back to England.

She bit into her bottom lip. It'd take a miracle for him to do that. He'd want his wife by his side so that his people saw a united front. He'd want her to raise their children and be a dutiful wife.

But he was crazy to think she wanted that, too. She wanted her freedom back, wanted to do as she pleased with her life, which included making use of her education and having a career of her own. She'd dreamed of becoming an editor who found the next bestselling hit, the nugget of gold in the mountain of scripts that would touch countless readers.

She stepped out onto the deck and crossed her arms, a bitter twist to her lips. That her husband had taken all that away from her made her resent and despise him with a passion that was as strong as their sexual chemistry.

A brisk breeze pushed some hair over her face and she pushed the light sable length back with a hand, uncovering her eyes to see her husband wading from out of the sea. She gulped and her nipples pebbled. Despite her twisted emotions there was no denying he was hot, an Adonis who could have been sculpted by one of the finest artists to have ever lived on Earth.

For a minute she allowed her eyes to roam freely over him. Wide shoulders tapered to a narrow waist and powerful thighs, and tight abs that even from this distance showcased a tight musculature that any athlete would be proud of. That his fitness likely stemmed from his stamina in the bedroom wasn't something she wanted to acknowledge.

Her mouth dried as her gaze slipped along the thin trail of dark hair that started just above his navel and led down to his groin. *Hot damn.* His cock was large even after stepping out of icy-cold ocean water.

She sensed his stare on her and she jerked her eyes up to his smirking, knowing gaze. He lifted a hand and she half-lifted hers in return, before snatching it back to her side. She wasn't his obedient puppet. She never would be! Spinning away, she marched back inside the house.

She was never going to be a gullible bride who believed in happily ever after. Theirs was no fairytale. She'd never love Mahindar and that was the one choice he'd never manipulate, unlike their arranged marriage.

She rubbed her goose pimpled arms and stepped into the kitchen, where she spied a half-full cup of coffee. Perhaps a caffeine hit would brighten her mood. She flicked on the kettle just as Mahindar's tread sounded on the stairs. She turned as he stepped through the glass door.

His eyes flared. "You look...delectable."

She crossed her arms and lifted her chin, refusing to be flattered or surrender to an up-close-and-personal of *his* spectacular nakedness. "It seemed pointless in getting dressed."

He cocked a brow. "And why is that?"

"You want to impregnate me. I'm making it easier for you."

He rubbed a hand over his face. "I want to make love to you. I don't care if we don't have children for the next few years at least."

She stalked toward him. "And yet I might be pregnant even now."

His eyes darkened. "And how does that make you feel?"

"Why would my feelings matter?" she asked sweetly. She stopped just in front of him, doing her best to not succumb after all and ogle his salt-dried golden skin, damp hair and hard body with its even harder cock. "When have they ever mattered? I've never had a choice in any of this...why start now?"

He clapped a hand around her forearm and jerked her close. "You're making a mockery of our wedding vows," he said softly, but with such dangerous undercurrents she couldn't help but shiver.

"Are you saying you meant them?"

A pulse throbbed in his jaw. "Are you saying you didn't?"

She gaped up at him, her mouth dry and her pulse galloping. "I don't love you," she croaked. "My vows were empty."

"Then allow me to change your mind," he snarled, before his mouth covered hers in a kiss that bordered on violent.

That she responded to his wildness, his pent up fury that matched her own wasn't relevant in that moment. All that mattered was the release of carnal need and high emotion.

His mouth was relentless as he kissed her and she moaned against his skilled lips, unaware he'd spun her around and marched her out onto the deck until the railing was against her spine and the brisk air and late midday sun went straight through her gossamer thin robe.

He tore his mouth from hers and looked down at her. "Turn around," he commanded.

She blinked. "Wh-what?"

"Turn around," he repeated. "I want to take you from behind while you cling to the railing while I make you come."

She shook her head. "No."

His eyes glinted with the threat of reprisal. "No?" he repeated.

"It's too dangerous. I could fall."

His passionate mouth thinned. "Do you really think I'd allow that to happen? And don't pretend a little danger doesn't stimulate you. You're a passionate woman. It's time to embrace that side of you."

"I won't be forced!" she said in a shrill voice, hating that he was bringing out a side of her that had never been awakened by anyone else.

He lifted his hands and settled them on her shoulders, one hand then drifting down her arm, brushing over her hip and then untying the little belt around her waist. As her nightgown fluttered apart, he moved his hand down her stomach before he slipped it between her thighs.

She gasped unsteadily as he began to stroke her clit with just the right amount of pressure, ensuring all the strength drained out of her limbs and all the fight drained out of her system.

"Who said anything about force?" he asked silkily.

"I hate you," she gritted out, using every last bit of her strength to tell him the truth before an orgasm shuddered through her and she could barely stand let alone talk.

His eyes hardening, he said, "And yet your body can't deny it wants me. I'm only sorry that makes you so...vindictive."

He turned her around and pressed her so that she was bent against the railing. He didn't even need to flip up her nightgown, it was short enough to bare her ass, and his big hands caressed her cheeks, making her shudder again. That she was desperate for his touch only amplified her loathing.

"Tell me you want me inside you," he said gruffly. "Tell me you want me to fuck you."

"Go to hell!"

"Such a fighter," he mused darkly. "It seems a shame to waste all that energy on rebelling against me when you know you want me to take you out here, where cameras even now might be snapping pictures of the famous sheikh and sheikha fucking where anyone might see us." His voice lowered. "Or does that turn you on, *habibi?*"

She groaned, his words alone making her wet with invitation, her whole body screaming for ultimate release. "Just...get it over with," she snarled.

He pressed his hand to her saturated pussy, stroking her wet flesh with a little sound of triumph. "Not until you ask me nicely."

"Can you *please* fuck me now before someone spies on us and leaks photos to the damn press—"

She gasped and quivered with both passion and indignation as he pushed inside her in one long, deep stroke that bounced her against the railing, her startled gasp also filled with awe. She'd had no idea sex could be so...heavenly.

Leaning over the rail, with her breasts tipping free, she might as well be flying, soaring while her husband—her *husband!*—fucked her. He had a knack of making her forget how she hated him, how their marriage was a farce with no love between them.

But what did love matter when they were so good together physically, with their bodies in-synch even if their minds were far apart?

The friction was just shy of painfully delicious as his smooth strokes soon became rougher, harder, and he pounded her ever closer to an abyss that had nothing to do with the white sandy beach far below.

She was close...so close. Then he reached between her legs and found her sweet spot, his touch setting her off. She came hard, her shrill cry joined soon after by his long, low growling-grunt as his seed ejected deep inside her.

But if she expected him to disconnect from her, physically and emotionally, she was wrong. He bent over her, his big hands caressing her sweat-dampened skin and his warm lips trailing kisses along her nape.

A seagull called out as it wheeled above them, its wingtips flashing bright white under the hot sun, the deep azure waves glinting and sparkling.

Yet the spectacular visual was secondary, an afterthought compared to the man behind her whose touch even now sent her body into raptures, as though her wild orgasm was giving out aftershocks. His big hands wielded pleasure in all the right places, places that were now awakened and ultra-responsive, while his lips and his prickly jaw tantalized with its abrasive coarseness.

"Let's go inside," he murmured near her ear. "You're covered in goose bumps."

She nodded, too mortified to admit that he had been the one who'd manufactured them, not the brisk air rallying against the heat of the sun.

He stepped back and carefully detached from her, his grunt reinforcing her own separation anxiety. When they were together, she was able to pretend nothing else mattered. Apart they were separate in every way.

He reached for her hand, and hesitating for just a fraction of a second, she accepted his clasp and followed him into the kitchen.

"I was thinking a fruit salad for lunch," he suggested, nodding toward the fruit bowl overflowing with local produce. "Something light that will tide us over until dinner."

She was glad when he released her hand to cut up their lunch, it gave her the strength to tie up her belt and fight for some semblance of sanity. She wasn't hungry, she was mortified. She hated Mahindar, but he was right, her body loved him...obsessed over him.

"Sit," he said pleasantly, pulling out a chair for her at the dining table. She did as he asked, masking her petulance by accepting the bowl of fruit salad he placed in front of her ten minutes later.

She had to admit it was crazy that a sheikh was looking after her. He was a man whose every need was catered for and every wish was granted. His people would no doubt be shocked to see him so...attentive.

Despite telling herself she wasn't hungry, she polished off the sweet, succulent fruit. Sex had clearly stimulated her appetite. Mahindar stood and collected her bowl along with his and placed them on the sink. When he returned he took her hand. "Come."

Been there, done that.

She choked back sudden, hysterical laughter as she followed him into the bathroom. That she wasn't sure whether to be relieved or disappointed this time when they took a shower together and they weren't intimate meant she really was a mess of contractions.

Mahindar seemed focused on soaping her skin impersonally and washing her hair, then drying it and her body before drying off himself.

"I'm not a baby, I can manage," she muttered weakly, enjoying his attention despite everything.

"Humor me," he said. "All my life women have tripped over themselves to look after my every need. And now I'm enjoying looking after my wife."

She wouldn't think about his concubines or his past and present lovers. As his wife she'd be expected to turn a blind eye to that kind of goings on. And to object would look as though she cared, and she most certainly did *not* care!

After wrapping her in a big, white fluffy towel, he slung one around his hips and led her into the walk-in closet. He held up a slinky silver gown. "Dress up?" His other hand retrieved and held up sexy lingerie. "Or dress down?"

She shrugged negligently, tamping down a desire to dress up for dinner for her husband. "Dress down. After all, that *is* what I'm here for, is it not? A honeymoon where we fuck as much as possible to get me pregnant."

His jaw tightened. "We've already discussed this. Children aren't my priority, not yet."

"And yet I'm not on any contraception and you haven't once used condoms."

He sighed. "It often takes months or even years to conceive. But if we were blessed with a child earlier than expected I'd give him or her every bit of my love and devotion."

A pang went through her chest at his declaration. No matter how she felt about him, it was nice to believe he wouldn't be an uncaring father like hers had been. She lifted her chin. "Of course you'll be blessed. You married me for my bloodline so that our children will one day rule your country."

"*Our* country," he said succinctly. He sighed. "I'm not the big bad wolf here, Arabelle. I'm trying hard to make us work. I *want* our marriage to work."

She softened a little at his words. That he'd said her name like it was a benediction also hadn't gone unnoticed. And he was right, he *had* been trying. Most men of his ilk would have used much harsher ways to pull her into line.

She managed a smile. "Then the evening gown it is."

Chapter Eleven

Mahindar couldn't take his eyes off his wife, whose natural beauty was enhanced by the flames of the fireplace that crackled and spat, and the light of the candles he'd lit on the dining table. She was entrancing, her fiery, stubborn will only making him want her more.

That she looked so small and delicate in her silver evening gown as she wolfed down her meal, which had been brought to them by their jeep driver from a nearby local village woman renowned for her cooking, somehow added to her appeal. How many women had he known who counted calories and refused anything fatty or sweet?

He'd always been attracted more to those who knew what they wanted and lived life their own way. It was just a pity his wife didn't want him. And perhaps therein lay the challenge. Would his interest wane the moment she surrendered to him? Would he prefer her spitting and scratching like a she-cat to keep him amused and aroused?

No. He wouldn't want her to change anything *except* her mind on their marriage. He didn't want only to possess her body, her wanted to be intertwined with her mind and soul, too.

He wanted them to be partners for life.

The three or four hours they'd wiled away chatting out on the deck while drinking wine and waiting on dinner had only cemented his desire to be with her. She wasn't just beautiful and smart, she was driven, too. She possessed all the qualities he admired in a woman, qualities they'd both hopefully one day pass onto their children.

But she didn't just stimulate his mind. She'd refrained from putting on any underwear and he'd been semi-aroused even since. He loved how her nipples poked against the thin bodice of her dress, despite how the fireplace warmed up the chill night air. Loved the husky note in her voice that showed, she too, wasn't immune to their chemistry.

"This is amazing!" she said as she swallowed yet another mouthful of the homemade pasta with spiced lamb. He grinned as she patted her belly, then added wistfully, "My mother was a terrible cook. Even though I only lived in the palace with her and my father for eight years, I can still remember her occasional attempts to show my father she wasn't just a pretty English wife."

"Did your father berate her on the cooking?" he asked, watching her closely and keeping his tone neutral. If there was one thing he knew about Sheikh Abdul Al Hussam, it was his temper.

She smiled. "My mother could do no wrong his eyes. I think it pleased him that she made an effort to do something for him. He even ate whatever she presented him despite having his own Michelin Star chef."

Mahindar blinked. *Interesting.* Rumor had it that Arabelle's father had sent his daughter away to England to get her out of his sight, but Mahindar now wondered if Abdul had simply given into his wife's request to have Arabelle educated elsewhere. If that was true, Abdul must truly love his wife. Few sheikhs allowed their daughters to be influenced and corrupted by foreigners.

He'd bet even his closest sheikh friends—Fayez, Jamal and Hamid—would never consider such an idea despite their own western educations. He resisted snorting. Not that he could talk. He couldn't imagine sending any of his kin away, especially at such a young and tender age.

"Enough about me," she said, her eyes suddenly watchful. "What were your parents like? Did they treat you well?"

His stomach tightened. Did she really need to learn about his distasteful childhood, where he'd grown up determined to be the opposite of his parents?

She blinked at him as the silence lengthened. "It can't have been so terrible, not with the way you've turned out."

"Oh?" he prompted.

She blushed, her paler skin offsetting her dark sable hair with its natural reddish-brown highlights. "You've turned a war-torn, long-suffering country into something...admirable. And from all accounts, your people have never been happier." She dabbed at her mouth with a napkin. "Though that might have changed now you've married me, a foreign girl despite my sheikh father."

His lips tilted at the corners. "And that bothers you?"

She tossed her head, reminding him of a hot-blooded, temperamental filly. "Of course not!" she denied. "You arranged the marriage with my father. I had no say in the matter. Your people can accept or reject me, it hardly matters either way."

"And yet I can see that it does," he said softly.

The sparks in her blue-green eyes were as clear as those in the fireplace. "Then you're seeing what you want to see."

She threw her napkin to the table and rose from her seat. "If you don't mind, I think I'd like to retire to bed now."

"You're asking permission to leave?" he asked, no longer restraining a wide smile. "You're becoming quite the malleable bride."

Her plump, kissable lips tightened into a thin line. "I'm not the docile, obedient wife you no doubt expected. I never will be."

He pushed to his feet, towering over her even in her heels. But she didn't look one bit intimidated, even tilting her head back there was heat in her stare, the same passion that excited and aroused him. "I was going to offer dessert," he murmured. "But bed sounds like a much better idea."

"Dessert?" She licked her lips, as though she was more interested in a sweet treat than she was in having sex. "W-what dessert do you have?"

He forced his mind out of the fantasy filling his head which involved her lips and her tongue on his body, and croaked, "Kunafa."

She patted a hand on her stomach. "I haven't tasted that since I was a little girl."

He smiled. "Then allow me to get you some before it goes cold."

She sat. "Thank you."

When he returned and sat in a chair next to her, placing a plate onto the table with one spoon and a chunk big enough to share, her eyes widened.

He used a fork to break off a piece and her mouth opened as she accepted his proffering, her eyes then sliding closed along with her mouth as she savored the food that would no doubt be nostalgic. "Mm."

He pushed the fork back into the pastry with its sugary filling and pistachio top, the tantalizing scent of citrus and rose water filling the air. He closed his mouth over the bite-sized piece even as her eyes fluttered open again and she watched him suck the prongs clean.

"More?" he asked huskily.

She nodded. "Please."

He proffered her another piece and this time she held his gaze as she sucked the dessert into her mouth, leaving the tines just as clean when he withdrew the fork.

He smothered a groan as he imagined her mouth wrapped around his cock and sucking him dry. He dropped the fork with a clank onto the plate next to what remained of their dessert, then leaned forward and claimed her mouth with his own.

He thought she might resist. Instead she moaned softly and kissed him back, their sweet breaths merging even as he stood and lifted her against him, then strode into their bedroom.

His bride mightn't love him but her body most certainly did. And he'd use every trick in his arsenal to make her change her mind. He broke the kiss to lay her onto the bed and follow her down. Her eyes gleamed in the weak moonlight seeping into the bedroom, her lips plumped with passion and her breaths erratic.

That he was also desperate to fuck her—and was too often consumed by thoughts of fucking her—was a lucky fringe benefit.

Chapter Twelve

Arabelle was still catching her breath an hour later, her senses reawakened and her whole body buzzing yet gratified all at once.

One thing she could say about her husband, he knew how to please a woman in bed. He wasn't just in it for his own release.

But then she'd been close to coming the moment he'd ripped off her gown like a caveman, then licked and sucked her nipples. When he'd done the same to her pussy, his stubble grazing her sensitive flesh, she'd tipped right over the edge. Then he'd slid his cock deep inside her, and she'd held his gaze as he'd rocked in and out, faster and faster, making her forget her every good intention as passion took hold and she'd shattered hard, taking him with her.

What was wrong with her? She'd been pleased when her mind had shut down despite her body's need for gratification. But she could no longer deny her mind and body were as one...at least when it came to sex.

The mattress creaked as he stood, gloriously naked, the trickle of moonlight filtering inside providing enough illumination to showcase his hard male body. He was lean and fit, with corded muscles she wanted to touch and trace, his golden skin drawing her eyes like a magnet.

He pulled back the covers, then took her hands and set her onto her feet. "Time for sleep," he said huskily.

She looked up at him. She'd always been short compared to most other people, but he made her feel tiny and even a little fragile in comparison. She didn't doubt for one second the promise he'd made into her ear while he'd been stroking in and out of her.

Next time I'll hold you against the wall and claim you.

But then she'd never doubted his strength. She'd only ever doubted his intentions for marrying her.

It didn't stop her from asking, "Will you stay with me this time?"

"Of course." His white teeth glinted in the semi-darkness. "I have to get some sleep eventually."

She climbed under the covers and he followed her and pulled her against his hardness, the tantalizing scent of sex and amber filling her nostrils. Then he drew the bedding around them and kissed her nape, murmuring, "Goodnight, my sweet little wife."

"Goodnight," she said in return, smiling wryly into the shadows knowing his embrace made her feel safe and secure.

As her eyes drifted shut, a vivid memory immediately penetrated her dreams...

The aroma of coffee beans lingered in Arabelle's nostrils, the air brisk outside and the earlier rain a wet shadow on the pavement as she and her friends left the coffee shop.

Her nape prickled, and hiding a frown, she glanced over her shoulder. But the lunchtime crowd was too dense to pick out any one person.

"Are you okay, honey?" Kiki asked, touching her shoulder with one of her long-nailed hands.

Arabelle nodded. "Yes, I'm fine." She forced a smile. "I guess with the end of year exams coming up I've been a bit overwhelmed."

Scott exhaled with disbelief. "You ace *all* your exams! You have nothing to be worried about. Me, on the other hand..."

Kiki's hair shook as she giggled. "I probably shouldn't laugh, but you're right, Scott. If anyone should be worried, it's you."

Scott waggled his eyebrows. "Except I have a tutor now." He glanced meaningfully at Arabelle. "And I foresee passing all my future exams with flying colors."

"Any excuse to get close to the one girl whose heart you haven't broken," Kiki trilled.

But Arabelle was barely listening. All her senses buzzed with the sensation of someone watching her, perhaps even listening in on the conversation with her friends. She twisted to look behind her once again, her eyes connecting like radar to a man whose black eyes glinted with brilliance and something deeper...something she couldn't quite read.

Contempt? Desire? No, something in-between.

That most of his face was hidden in shadow by a stylish hat still didn't quite hide his Middle Eastern heritage or the expensive suit that very few English men could afford. Her stomach roiled. Had her father sent someone to spy on her?

Then the man turned, and even with his great height he was soon lost in the crowd. She inhaled sharply, filling her lungs with air once again even as her friends called out, "Arabelle, what are you doing? Let's go!"

Her jaw ached as she pasted on a fake smile and ran to catch up. But her senses were left reeling from the confrontation with the stranger, a man her mind wouldn't let go of.

A man who'd been a stranger and who was now all too familiar.

Her dream faded to reality. And as she jerked awake, her mind shouted *Mahindar!*

Chapter Thirteen

Arabelle leaned against the high deck railing, the sun rising over the ocean's horizon while the salt-laden and bracing sea breeze did its best to clear her mind. Until her husband's tread sounded from behind.

She stiffened, but then his big body was behind her, his heat emanating her like a blanket even before his arms wrapped around her and he nuzzled her neck. "What are you doing out here all alone when you could be in bed with me?" he murmured.

Despite the thin white shift she'd thrown on that did absolutely nothing to keep her warm, her shivers weren't from the cold. Her body was already succumbing to his touch, drawn to him like barren ground was to rain.

It would be so easy to melt against him, to pretend she didn't know about him trailing her all those months ago, no doubt to see if she was worthy enough to be his bride.

She hated the subterfuge, the secrets and the lies when a part of her had been drawn to Mahindar's brutal honesty. She twisted in his arms and swallowed hard at seeing all his...nakedness. She forced her gaze upward, away from his long, hard cock that made her mouth water no matter what her mind told her body.

She blinked, aware his height along with his dark, brilliant gaze was unmistakable now as one and the same from her past. That he hadn't been completely honest with her was like a knife in the back. She might despise him but she'd believed in him and had never imagined he'd lie, not even by omission.

That her chest ached and her stomach felt hollowed out only added to the pain of his betrayal.

His gaze narrowed. Then he tucked his hand beneath her chin and asked, "What's wrong?"

She refused to tell him, not until she was ready. It didn't stop a reckless need to antagonize him. "Other than being trapped in a marriage I don't want?"

His nostrils flared and his eyes sparked. That his voice stayed calm and reasonable intimidated her more than she wanted to acknowledge when he said, "I showed you leniency when you ran away, far more than I might have."

"I guess I haven't been mistreated," she acknowledged, "although many would argue that taking away my freedom is the worst form of abuse."

His eyes turned speculative. "What *is* freedom?"

"It's the ability to choose what we want from our life, to be who we want and shape our own future."

"And you can't do that as my wife? Can you not see the endless opportunities you have now as sheikha to a people who want only to admire and respect you?"

She stared at him, trying to read the intensity of his gaze. "Why wouldn't they admire and respect me now?"

His smooth brow furrowed. "All they've seen is a bride who ran away and abandoned them before the ink had dried on the marriage certificate. A sheikha who is insolent and reckless. A sheikha who appears to have no regard or staying power for a country that is peaceful and prosperous."

She blinked. "They know I ran away?"

He shrugged. "Rumors spread even with the threat of punishment. You can only blanket the gossip now by showing our people that your inner goodness far outweighs any misguided bad."

"You preach to me like you've done no wrong." She glared a little. "Like you've never lied to me."

"Why do I get the feeling you're going somewhere with this?'

"Guilt, perhaps?" she mocked. Then she added bitterly, "Remorse for the fact you were spying on me long before we met at the altar?"

He exhaled slowly. "So you do remember me."

"I didn't until I dreamed about you last night. You were the man who followed me after I stepped outside of the coffee shop with my friends. The same man I'd sensed at least a handful of times beforehand." Her hands clenched. "Tell me I'm wrong!"

"I never once lied about it," he replied. "I needed a wife, but I wasn't going to accept just anyone, no matter the bloodline. Then I took one look at you, at your glorious vivacity and inner strength, and I knew I had to make you mine."

"But I didn't want to be yours! I will *never* want to be yours."

"You don't know that," he said quietly, but with more dangerous intensity in his words than if he'd roared them at her.

Her bottom lip trembled. "You could have at least introduced yourself, allowed me to get to know you." Her voice trembled, too, as she added, "I might even have liked you!"

His smile hinted at sadness. "Yet that first time you saw me you clearly didn't want to know me. Despite my Middle Eastern looks, I was a foreigner to you, a stranger. I knew right away not to approach you again when we'd have the rest of our lives to get to know one another."

"That was your choice. Where was *my* choice in all of this?" she said shakily.

He dragged a hand over his face. "Let me show you something."

She wanted to continue challenging him. Instead she asked, "Now?"

He glanced down at her transparent shift and his own nakedness, a reluctant smile creasing his face. "Once we're dressed."

It took everything she had not to gawp at his tight ass and corded thighs, his back muscles that flexed and shifted lightly with each stride as she followed him into the shared walk-in closet.

She had to swallow her disappointment when he pulled on casual jeans and a gray polo shirt. She picked out white cuffed pants, an emerald green t-shirt with appliqued anchor, and simple canvas shoes with an inbuilt, squishy memory foam that pillowed her feet.

She'd gotten used to the stipend her father had sent her and had grown accustomed to cheap bargain clothes. What she wore now might be casual wear but there was nothing casual in the expensive fabrics and expert stitching.

Though there were also drawers full of jewelry she ignored them and instead secured her hair into a topknot, leaving her neck and ears bare.

"Coffee before we go?" her husband asked.

"Yes, please."

She followed him into the kitchen, and he added, "I should have installed a coffee machine. But on the rare occasions I actually stay here, I figured it wasn't a big deal to have instant."

"I don't mind instant," she conceded. "I'm used to the taste. And I found it made my few outings to the coffee shops in England extra special."

His shoulders tightened a little as he flicked on the kettle and grabbed some mugs. "You appeared to have a tight group of friends there."

"I did," she conceded. "I wonder what they must think now that I've disappeared off the face of the Earth."

"They will no doubt imagine the worst."

"My departure *was* rather abrupt."

"Your father isn't known for his...sensitivity," Mahindar conceded. He spooned coffee into the mugs and asked, "Do you miss your friends?"

"Of course." She sat into a high-backed stool that was a clone to three others pushed under the overhang of a dark-swirled marble island countertop. "They've probably started their careers now. Kiki had an offer for her journalism degree and I was contemplating an editing and acquisitions role in a major publishing house."

The kettle boiled and clicked off and silence filled the void before her husband asked softly, "You had your future all set out in front of you."

She nodded. "I did."

His gaze didn't move from her. "Do you think, one day, you might be happy with your new future?'

She blinked and sighed. "I honestly don't know."

He poured the boiled water into their mugs then added in a little milk and sugar as he stirred. "I regret that I took away your dream."

"Me too," she said in a small voice. "When I left Lumana and my family behind to live in a whole new country with a whole new language I was scared to death. But I soon adapted. I studied hard to learn English and I soon fell in love with the language and the written word. I knew soon after I wanted to be a part of that."

"And now?"

"And now...nothing. It is a useless skill here."

His jaw clenched a little. "You have talent. There is no need for you to waste it."

She accepted her drink and took a big mouthful. "It's a little late for that."

"It's never too late to pursue a passion." Mahindar watched her closely then as he, too, drank his coffee. "What of your friend, Scott?"

She shrugged, but the atmosphere was suddenly tense. Mahindar no doubt assumed Scott was the man she left behind and who still had her heart. That she loved no man wasn't up for discussion. She'd have to live with her lie. "I have no doubt he'll go on and help run his dad's publishing house. He was groomed for that role whether he liked it or not."

She bit her bottom lip. She was such a hypocrite accusing her husband of lying when she'd done the same herself by pretending to love someone in England.

"So your UK friends aren't truly free, either," Mahindar asked.

She narrowed her eyes. "Scott still has a choice. I think he just accepted the easy route knowing he was yet to find his passion in life."

"So his passion wasn't you?" Mahindar asked smoothly.

She placed her mug down on the bench with a clack. "Scott had many lovers. I wasn't one of them. I think he liked the chase as much as he did the final act in the bedroom."

Mahindar expelled a slow breath, his shoulders loosening. "So he failed with you. I bet he hated you were in love with another man."

She shook her head, her voice cracking. "I guess I'll never know. Not that I ever imagined I would end up returning to the Middle East, as a bride no less, to a sheikh."

Her husband's eyes glowed. "You must hate that I brought you here without first making love to the man of your heart."

She swallowed. Her one little lie was getting too deeply entrenched. But she refused to add more to it. Silence was the far safer option.

When she didn't answer he ran a hand over his face. "I honestly never cared if you were a virgin or not. But purity *is* considered a rare prize in Rajhabi as much as it is in Lumana," he conceded softly. "I truly believe you were fated to be mine."

"Then it was your fate. It was never mine."

"Only time will tell." Before she could argue some more, he put his mug down and said decisively, "Let's get breakfast."

She drank the last of her coffee and glanced out one of the front windows which showed the ramp that connected to a small driveway outside, and the road that continued past. No car waited for them. "Are we waiting for a driver?"'

"No. We'll stroll along the beach if you're up for it."

THE SHEIKH'S RUNAWAY BRIDE   67

She placed her mug in the sink, intrigued. Were they having a picnic breakfast on the beach? "I'd like that."

The strong coffee had revived her, left her feeling a little more optimistic after her bald faced lie, and she followed him outside on the high deck and down its stairs, breathing deep of the salty air.

The sand squeaked under their shoes and a faint breeze played with the strands of her hair she'd left out of the topknot. Though his hand loosely held hers, there was serious strength in his fingers along with some rough calluses on his skin that told her he didn't just sign paperwork to rule his country.

"Where are we going?" she asked, squinting a little at the gleaming swathe of sand that continued onward for miles without a single other person to be seen.

"I wanted you to meet someone."

"Oh?"

He nodded. "A lovely old woman who chose to live outside the village." He chuckled. "She's...different, but I think you'll like her and understand her better than most people might."

Ten minutes later they veered off the beach and up an embankment with a light track that had been packed down over time by regular walks. Following the trail through some palms and hardy coastal trees they came to a hut where half a dozen chickens scratched in the sand near its veranda.

A rocking chair sat empty beside a little round table with a teapot, while the scent of wood smoke filled the air, its white haze curling into the sky from a crooked chimney.

Mahindar smiled. "Let's hope she's in the mood for some company."

The door opened and a small figure appeared in the doorway, an old, hunched over woman who looked at them through nut-brown eyes that were dulled by age but sharp with intelligence. "Who is it?"

she called out. She shaded her eyes with a shaky hand. "Is that you, Mahindar?"

He chuckled. "Yes, Aisha. Who else would dare visit you here?"

"Who else indeed!" the old woman chuckled. She shuffled out onto the veranda and down the trio of steps, the chickens flapping out of her way with indignant clucks. "I hope you're here to share some arrack with me. As you said, visitors here and few and far between."

"To be fair, we both know that is your choice, Aisha."

"So it is," she conceded and stepped into his arms for a hug that looked comical with her so tiny and frail and Mahindar so tall and powerful. "And you know I wouldn't have it any other way."

Mahindar smiled down at her. "Bit early in the day for Arrack."

"Then you'd better have some of my fish stew first. I know how much you enjoy it."

"I hoped you might say that," Mahindar informed with a smile. "But please, let me first introduce you to my wife. Sheikha Arabelle. Arabelle, meet our neighbor and friend, Aisha."

"Such a pleasure to meet you," Arabelle said with a smile.

Aisha cackled again. "Oh, aren't you a lovely one. And his wife, no less! I never thought I'd see the day!"

"It just took the right woman, Aisha," Mahindar said in a teasing voice that held a somber note.

Aisha looked her up and down. "I believe you're right. She's no shrinking violet. She's just what you need."

Mahindar chuckled as he followed Aisha into her home, clasping Arabelle's hand even as he ducked in the doorway and drew her into the surprisingly tidy hut with its bamboo floors and tiny kitchen and lounge room.

A big pot sat on the gas stove where a flame just barely flickered with enough heat to keep the fish stew inside it warm. Aisha explained, "I keep the gas lit all day to keep the pot barely simmering. It's had all the flavors you could imagine from various vegetables and meats over the years. I simply add the stock, herbs, vegetables and whatever protein I'm eating for the day and reuse the master stock the next day. And so on."

Arabelle was intrigued. She'd heard of the process, unlike anybody who lived in the western world who would throw out leftovers after a day or two. It would be frowned upon and thought unhygienic to reuse stock time and time again.

She inhaled the complex scent that suddenly infiltrated the home. "It smells divine."

Aisha clapped her leathery hands. "Good. Good. You will try some?"

"I'd love to," she said with a smile, accepting the seat her husband pulled out for her at the four seater square table. There was nowhere else one could eat. The single armchair in front of a laptop on a little desk was clearly for Aisha alone.

Minutes later a bowl of fish stew was placed in front of her and Mahindar, a basket of homemade bread rolls put into the center of the table along with a big jug of what was probably the date arrak she appeared to enjoy.

Aisha sat and grinned. "Let's eat!"

Chapter Fourteen

Arabelle leaned back and patted her stomach. "That was delicious." She smiled at Aisha. "Thank you for you hospitality."

Aisha grinned, her already thin lips almost disappearing. "Oh shush, dear girl. It was the least I could do. If it wasn't for Mahindar I wouldn't be here right now."

He sighed and placed his spoon into his bowl as he looked at the older woman. "You know how I feel about that."

Aisha cackled. "Oh, you and your silly guilt. If it wasn't for you I'd probably be imprisoned back in the same gilded palace I ran away from. Except I have no doubt I'd be in chains with bloodied whip marks on my back."

"And I would have started a war to get you back."

Aisha cackled. "A war that would kill many innocents to save one? I'm flattered my dear boy, but neither of us wants that. Better that I hide away here in paradise than risk anyone else getting hurt in my dear husband's quest for revenge."

Mahindra nodded. "This house was only ever meant to be temporary. I never wanted you to stay so isolated and alone all these years. You could have at least lived in the village."

Aisha shook her head. "You know how people talk and gossip spreads. I might have been tracked down. No, thank you. I live a simple life and I couldn't be happier for it."

Arabelle blinked at Mahindar. "So you helped Aisha escape from an arranged marriage while agreeing to one yourself?"

Aisha shook her head. "Your husband wasn't even alive when I was forced to marry fifty-six years ago. I was sixteen when I wed Sheikh

Ramirez who was two years older than me, and who already had three wives." She sighed and looked into the distance. "I managed to escape after enduring my husband's sick cruelty for too many years. But I was fast running out of places to hide and people to trust when Mahindar brought me here to live out my years in peace."

"So you were on the run until recently?" Arabelle asked.

Aisha nodded. "Until a decade ago. It wasn't fun, but I did meet some good men in that time, many of whom might have sheltered me if I'd asked. But I couldn't risk their lives. Still...I'd do it all over again than be forced into a lifetime of terror."

"I'm sorry for what you went through."

Aisha leaned forward and grasped Arabelle's hand with bony fingers. "Don't be sorry for me. I'm happy now. I just hope you're happy too. Unlike my husband, Mahindar is a kind and generous man."

He looked away, as though uncomfortable with the praise.

So he should be! All Arabelle had ever wanted was to fall in love with someone of her choice, not have that choice made for her! But he'd taken that away from her as well as her career before it had even began. "I don't have my freedom, either."

Aisha cackled again and swept a hand out. "You'd prefer to on the run and, at best, live like this? Don't get me wrong, I love it here. I get to hear the gentle swish of the waves every night that sometimes become a roar. I get to breathe in the salty tang of natural air. I get to live life on my terms. But I also live in constant fear that one day I might have all that taken away from me."

"Shouldn't your husband have given up by now? Surely time has dimmed his need for vengeance?"

Aisha shook her head. "Not at all. In fact I'd say quite the opposite. I'm the wife—his whore, as he so eloquently puts it—who ran off and humiliated him in front of his people. That I was never caught and trialed for my sins would be nothing short of salt rubbed into a wound, one that festers each and every day I'm not found."

"I'm sorry," Arabelle said softly, "if there was some way I could help you, I would."

Mahindar looked at her, his expression thoughtful.

"Thank you, I do believe you mean that. Honestly though, just be thankful for the husband you have. Freedom will come to you, too, once you accept that fate brought you together." She released Arabelle's hand to pour them some arrak. "Enough about me, though. Let's take our drinks onto the beach. I want to hear all about you two."

A couple of hours later, Arabelle walked with Mahindar back to his holiday house. It had been lovely sitting on the beach with their drinks, which Aisha had topped up from a jug. And despite having breakfast Arabelle was a little lightheaded and foolishly happy.

It had been nice to see her husband so relaxed, his hand clasping hers and their toes digging in the sand side-by-side. It had been clear the weight of his country wasn't a burden sitting heavily on his shoulders. In fact he could have been any man sitting on the beach with his woman.

Passersby, if there had been any, would have had no clue they all three were royalty.

But Arabelle would not be alone now in seeing Mahindar's set jaw and heavy silence. "You risk a lot by hiding Aisha on your island."

"Some things are worth the risk." He glanced at her as he reached for her hand and intertwined his fingers around hers. "Not everything has to be about profit or glory."

"Then why marry me?"

He turned to her, his eyes holding hers. "You really need to ask that?"

"Yeah, I do." She lifted her free hand to brush some tendrils of hair out of her eyes, the sun hot on her face. "I always thought I'd marry a man of my choosing, a man I loved."

His eyes looked pained at first, then fierce. "Is there no chance that I might be that man you love?"

She blinked, feeling oddly numb. "If there had been any chance of that happening it's gone now. You took away my choice, my freedom, and along with it, any admiration and high regard I might have had for you."

"You've been brought up in the western world and its ideals, I understand that, but don't disregard or throw away the life we could have together."

"A forced marriage shouldn't be tolerated in *any* culture," she snapped.

He sighed heavily. "We can't change what has already happened, *habibi*. But we can look ahead to our future."

He sounded so sincere and so committed in doing just that, her body unwittingly swayed toward his. She jerked back, dismayed by her physical weakness toward him. "No apology? No regrets?" she asked bitterly.

He shook his head. "Why apologize for something I wouldn't change? I desired you as my bride, and now I have you by my side as my sheikha, my wife." He leaned close, his voice seductive and dark, "And I wouldn't have it any other way."

It was crazy the way her heart thumped, not in shocked outrage, but something closer to passion and need. She swallowed past her thick throat. "I thought you were better than this. I thought you were a sheikh who was above those outdated traditions that see women treated like objects, like assets."

"I'm bringing about change," he said gently. "But I refuse to force my people in abandoning their time-honored customs. I'm nudging their mindset to what I believe will be a better future, not ripping their beliefs out of their heads as though the past means nothing."

"And what of my beliefs? My mindset? My past and my future?"

He tugged her closer, his bent head inches from hers. "Share it all with me," he said intently. "Make me a part of your life and together we can make this country even better."

His mouth was so damn close to hers, his lips that had redefined her opinion on kissing. Lips that had brought her to orgasm along with his—

She shook her head and stepped back, pulling her hand free. If she wasn't careful she'd be following him around like a lovesick, sex-addicted fool. "You have advisors for that."

He nodded sagely. "I do." He crossed his arms. "But they are all men."

She scowled. "Let me guess...no woman has been willing to step into such an exalted position for fear of reprisal?"

"No woman has even applied for that position."

"And yet how many years ago did England vote in a woman prime minister?"

His eyes narrowed speculatively. "England isn't your country. Rajhabi is."

"Says you," she said bitterly. "If home is where the heart then I am British through and through."

"Your heart is mine, *habibi*. I will see to that."

The warmth flooding through her wasn't entirely from the sun. She glanced away from him, doing her best to regain some semblance of clarity. Except the inner glow left her so messed up she had no comeback, no...nothing. When she finally looked back at him she asked, "Is this how all your sheikh friends operate to get a woman?"

He threw his head back and laughed. "Fayez, Jamal and Hamid already have more women than they know what to do with." He sobered. "In all honesty, though, I think if the right woman came along, all three of them would be lost. I only hope Hamid finds that right woman sooner rather than later."

She recalled the flamboyant and rather inebriated Hamid at her and Mahindar's reception. The man had reminded her more of a Johnny Depp pirate than any sheikh she'd met. There had been something compelling about him, something wild and wanton that many women would find irresistible.

Not that she'd felt a spark with him—with any of Mahindar's good looking friends—but she imagined plenty of women went weak at the knees at seeing them.

Meanwhile her senses had been overloaded by her husband. She'd been intoxicated by his power, overwhelmed by his good looks, his height and strength, and his dark gaze that showcased his brilliant mind.

She'd never been so aware of a man before in her life. She'd told herself it was because he was her husband now, and of course her senses were alert around him. That he was the man she was expected to spend the rest of her life with, whether she wanted to or not, was irrelevant.

Her body's awareness sent her into a tailspin. She didn't want to want him. She wanted her old life back along with her friends, but most of all she wanted the career she'd studied hard for and had yet to begin.

"Let's get back," he said in a gentler tone. "Lunch is waiting for us."

Chapter Fifteen

She'd been expected some salad with some cold meats, instead she followed Mahindar inside to a dining table that was groaning with seafood, roast meat, salads and baked vegetables. Then he pointed to the beef wellington, a pastry wrapped meat that was famous in England.

"I thought you might have gotten a little homesick for it by now."

She clapped her hands. "That is my favorite British food. How did you know?"

He arched a brow. "There is little I don't know about you."

They washed up in the bathroom while she digested his words. He didn't know everything about her. He hadn't known she was virgin. She was kind of glad to give him that one surprise.

Back in the dining room he pulled out a chair for her. She sat and had already piled her plate high when he sat opposite her.

"Hungry?" he asked with a grin.

She nodded. "I do like to eat."

She was bursting at the seams by the time she finally pushed her plate away and said, "I can't eat another bite."

He chuckled. "Well let's put what we want away for dinner. The rest I'll send back to the village. I'm sure they'll make a celebration out of it."

"Oh? Why aren't we celebrating with them?"

His eyes gleamed. "I thought you might like some alone time with your husband."

That was the last thing she wanted. She needed space away from where sex didn't hover enticingly between them and churn her emotions into a battlefield between hate and desire. "We have the rest of our lives for that."

His white teeth dazzled behind the dark scruff on his face, sending her stomach pitching with a whole different kind of need. He stroked his jaw and murmured, "In that case I'm sure I could organize something."

The jeep that had taken them from the airport arrived not even an hour later, its driver and three other men dutifully retrieving all the remaining food, except for the beef wellington, and placing it into the back of the jeep.

One young man with blond hair, green eyes and a ready smile threw Arabelle admiring glances. The driver eventually cuffed him on the side of the head, but the blond surfer-dude lookalike didn't look one bit chastised.

Arabelle ignored him. She had more than enough gorgeous masculinity and testosterone in her husband. "Should we invite Aisha? She must get lonely by herself all the time."

She was vaguely aware of the blond man's gaze behind her when Mahindar shook his head. "She doesn't like crowds, and she feels safe where she is."

"You're probably right." She looked around, but the blond man had already averted his eyes and grabbed the last of the food. No doubt Mahindar's imposing stare had sent him running for cover.

She hid a grin and got busy cleaning up the few dishes they'd used. She was at the sink when Mahindar gave the driver some last minute instructions near the front door. She sensed her husband behind her then even before he wrapped his arms around her waist and bent his head to whisper in her ear.

"I don't want my wife doing dishes."

"And I don't want to be waited on hand and foot." She turned in his arms and lifted her sudsy hands to his face. "I'll never be the pampered princess you expect me to be."

His eyes darkened and he groaned, his mouth covering hers, dominating the kiss until the moment she responded and inched her wet hands behind his nape. His lips softened, coaxing her into complete submission.

Oh, god.

Even if she'd found the strength she couldn't have shut down her body's response. His touch charged her, turned her body into an electric current that zinged right through her. A charge that went straight to full throttle and seemingly charged him, too.

He spun her around and lifted her so that she was sitting on the island countertop, their mouths still fused as he continued kissing her while pulling her hair free. Only when he pulled his head back and gazed at her unbound hair and her ripe lips did he mutter, "So damn beautiful."

His words were like a trigger that released all her inhibitions. She reached for him and stripped off his clothes as he stripped off hers. His shirt went first, then her pants and thong. He tugged off her T-shirt and unclipped her bra and threw it aside while she unzipped his fly and pushed his button undone. He didn't bother to fully take off his jeans. There was no need when he was commando.

With nothing other than the gentle swell of the waves hitting the shore outside, their panting breaths and groans was the only exotic music they needed, their desire a pressure cooker as they came together again.

He clasped her thighs and pushed them wide, dragging her to the edge of the countertop before he stepped between her legs. With a groan, he one-handed his cock and guided it to her core, and his eyes holding hers, he plunged inside her, his shaft a spear that filled her and had her gripping onto his shoulders, her head falling back and her hair trailing behind her.

When he began thrusting slow and deep, she locked her legs around his hips and bucked against him. *Holy fuck.* If slow and deep touched all her delicious keynotes, then fast and hard must surely hit all the high notes.

She wanted wild and wanton. She even wanted a little pain with the pleasure.

He responded as though he'd read her mind.

He pulled out, flipped her around so that she was sprawled over the granite top, then he was driving in and out of her like theirs was the last sexual act they'd ever have together.

He sucked on her nape, his sweat-slicked chest pressing against her back, his nuts slapping her butt and his groan mingling with her cries of delight while his amber scent intoxicated her as she inhaled deep.

"I'm. So. Close!" she gasped.

"So am I, baby," he growled, reaching past her butt to finger the hard pearl between her thighs that rejoiced at his deft touch.

She stiffened, then shattered hard, her inner muscles clamping hold around him. "Holy shit!" she screamed, her orgasm propelling her into outer body dizzying heights before she floated for long, glorious seconds into sublime bliss.

That Mahindar had exploded a second after her only barely registered, as did the warmth of his seed flooding inside her.

This might be the night he makes me pregnant...if I'm not already.

The thought drifted hazily through her head even as Mahindar carefully dislodged from her then turned her around and picked her up.

"Why don't you sleep for a little while," he suggested huskily. "We both can. We have a few hours before the village celebrations."

She smiled, nodded, then her eyelids drifted shut as he placed her on the bed. She was vaguely aware of his weight depressing the mattress next to her, and of the covers drifting over and his arms wrapping around her...then nothing.

Chapter Sixteen

They arrived in the backseat of the jeep at the same fishing village they'd passed the first day of their honeymoon. Tables and chairs had been set up on the pier with fairy lights strung along the railings and the scent of citronella from squat candles filling the air.

The driver opened Mahindar's passenger door and he nodded thanks before he strode around to open her other door. She smiled and clasped his hand, feeling more regal than she ever had as she stepped onto the dusty road in her silver heels beside the beach and pier.

Was her white, floaty dress too much for the occasion? She might feel all noble and regal but her naughtier side was getting off on the brazen sensuality of wearing nothing underneath except a brief thong.

But everything regal and naughty dissolved, a fluttery, sick feeling in her tummy overwhelming her as the villagers approached in an excited babble of greeting.

Would the villagers—Mahindar's people—like and accept her? Perhaps she'd instinctively asked to come here to test her mettle before facing the much harder-to-please people of Rajhabi?

Her worries soon proven unfounded when they were overrun with the sixty or seventy adults and children who congratulated them on their marriage, thanked them for their generous donation of food and finally welcomed them to their celebrations.

It was like being swept along by a wave as she and Mahindar kept pace with everyone else moving onto the pier. Someone pulled out a guitar and strummed beautiful music while Mahindar pulled out a seat for Arabelle at a table and sat next to her. She almost groaned at being faced with even more food, but politely accepted a glass of wine while she got her fingers greasy eating marinated chicken wings and pork ribs.

She spotted the surfer dude in the crowd, his blond hair and green eyes standing out amongst all the swarthy skin of the island natives with their dark eyes and glossy black hair. He winked at her but was soon lost in the crowd when a pair of young women vied for his attention and drew him away.

Arabelle got just as distracted by the conversation going on around them, which started off muted but soon grew in volume with the wine consumed alongside the food. The atmosphere was festive and fun and she chatted with Mahindar to the people around them, both laughing with a young, married couple whose two year old boy stamped his feet to the guitar music.

Mahindar leaned close and murmured, "You will make a great mom one day."

She turned to him, her throat drying. Children hadn't been on her agenda. All she'd wanted was a career with unlimited books to make her happy. "It shouldn't be too difficult when we have Nannies to rear them."

He frowned. "We will lead busy lives, there's no doubting that. But I don't want our children to have part-time parents. Nannies will be used mostly for those special occasions when we need them."

She blinked at him under the fairy lights, his serious face all too entrancing. Then a surge of bitterness hit front and center. It was all well and good for him to want a full time mother for his children. "So while you're running the country I'm running around after our children?"

His frown deepened. "Is that not the greatest honor?"

"If it was *you* would be doing it." She sighed heavily. "What does it matter of my opinion, anyway? I don't get a choice, either way."

His gaze turned considering. "I think you're determined to hate your role as sheikha."

"Do I need to remind you ours was an arranged marriage? One I didn't even have a say in. I'm finding it a little hard now to view my role as your wife in a positive light."

"You know arranged marriages are commonplace in our world. I'm not the bad guy you like to think I am."

"You could be a serial rapist for all I know." Not that he'd need to be with all the women at his damn disposal. She'd never forgive him for his harem, for those other women at his beck and call.

His eyes narrowed and his nostrils flared. But then few people would dare suggest such a thing. Her stomach knotted with sudden anxiety. Though a part of her knew his western education saw him more indulgent to her ways, she instinctively knew not to push too hard. Beneath his civilized, royal veneer beat the heart of a fierce barbarian.

"Then allow me to give you a brief character reference and bio."

She bit her bottom lip. "That isn't necessary."

"Oh, but it is, *habibi,* if we want to move forward."

She sighed, then said haughtily, "Very well."

His grim smile revealed he'd taken note of her royal decree. But if it bothered him he didn't let on. Hell, it probably put a bigger fire in his belly to make her a slave to his country.

"When I was conceived there was much celebration."

"Of course," she said drily.

He leaned closer. "I was considered quite the miracle baby after my mother had two stillborn children and three miscarriages."

She swallowed down sudden nausea. His mother had been a broodmare who'd kept on giving despite her obvious inability to carry to full term. "I'm sorry. I had no idea."

He didn't appear to acknowledge her apology. In fact he seemed lost in the past when he added, "I might have been hailed as a blessing, and was rather spoilt in many ways."

Why did she get a sudden, deep feeling he wasn't telling her everything? That his childhood wasn't some fairytale and was in fact rather brutal?

"But it didn't stop my parents dying far too young thanks to the war destroying our country and our people," he continued. "I was only eighteen when I took on the reign as sheikh."

"So young," she said softly. "Yet you managed to turn the war on its head."

He nodded. "Thanks to my success, all those revered whispers at my birth exploded into salutations."

He deserved nothing less.

She retrieved her wine glass and raised it in the air. "To many more blessings."

He smiled, his eyes assessing. "Perhaps, unlike my mother, we'll be blessed by many children."

He was insufferable! Yet she couldn't help but grin a little as she tipped the wine down her throat.

A middle-aged woman stood and walked to where the guitar player continued strumming. When she picked up a microphone and began to sing in a husky, crooning voice, Mahindar turned to Arabelle and said, "Let's dance."

One of the villagers shouted encouragement, and others joined in. With so many faces watching expectantly and her husband standing and proffering her a hand, she didn't have much choice.

She accepted his hand and stood gracefully, though it took more effort than it should with the wine leaving her warm and giddy inside. Mahindar led her close to the end of the pier and pulled her into his arms, the nearby singer and guitarist serenading them with a sweet love song.

With a shaky sigh of surrender, she leaned her head against her husband's chest, the strength of his heart beating like a rhythmic drum under her ear. How could she fight him...fight this? She might hate him but he made her feel...safe. It was seriously dumb to fall for his charms and his sexual expertise, but logic and intelligence had little to do with the way she felt in his arms.

With the melody flooding over them and his amber scent filling her nostrils along with the fresh, salty sea air, she might as well be in heaven. His big hands moved to clasp her lower back, his touch on her so right she couldn't help but look up at him with a smile.

He smiled in return, then bent his head to kiss her upturned mouth, his lips gentle but possessive. She heard some *oohs* behind them, as though the villagers were touched by the romance of their newly married sheikh and sheikha. But she was too caught up in the moment to worry about protocol and the fact she'd never wanted this marriage let alone be basking in her husband's attentions.

The guitarist slowed his strumming, the singer's voice becoming even more sultry and sexy, the evening as surreal and magical as Arabelle's chemistry with Mahindar.

He pulled back, his eyes glowing. "You were right in wanting to come here tonight."

"And you were right in agreeing to bring me here." She smiled. "Your people are lovely."

"And you are even lovelier," he murmured.

It should have been corny, but coming from her husband every word was sincere, heartfelt. Her face heated a little, but the cool, briny breeze that tickled her nape also helped to offset her flush.

He looked up. "A storm's brewing."

She blinked and tore her gaze away from him to look out to sea. The stars had disappeared on the horizon, the gentle waves that lapped at the shore already a little restless and choppy.

She sighed. "I don't want this night to end."

He lifted a hand and cupped the side of her face. "It doesn't have to end yet. We can watch the storm approach from the safety of our balcony."

A thrill shot up her spine at the thought of seeing the fury of Mother Nature while wrapped in the safety of Mahindar's arms. "I'd like that."

"Good," he murmured, "because I intend to make love to you while we watch the storm."

Her pulse beat a frantic tattoo at the side of her neck. "The lightning—"

"Will add to the intensity."

Oh, god. Her nipples pebbled beneath her flimsy excuse for a dress, its inbuilt bodice fabric doing little to disguise her yearning. That she was wet with lust was a secondary concern.

"Everyone is packing up," he mused with a smile. "The villagers know not to take any chances with Mother Nature."

She turned around. He was right. While she'd been lost in the moment between them, half the food had been cleared away, many hands making light work. She took a step toward them. "We should help."

His hand that clasped hers didn't release her. "No." she turned around with a frown, and he added, "They would be offended even if we offered." His eyes gleamed. "I've got a much better idea."

She didn't argue when he led her off the pier while the villagers scurried back and forth. They didn't appear to notice Mahindar leading her onto the beach and in the shadows beneath the pier, where waves chopped and thrashed halfway up the shore.

She turned to him with a frown. "Why—"

He pressed the palm of his hand to her mouth and bent to whisper in her ear, "I thought you might enjoy the show."

It was only then she realized they weren't alone under the pier. Someone gasped in the far shadows near a pillar. No. Not someone. *Three* someone's all tangled up kissing while stripping off their clothes.

Oh, my. Her stomach clenched, and her blood thickened and warmed, her imagination in overdrive and her stare unblinking. But as much as it turned her on she wouldn't ever partake in a threesome with her husband. Not even with someone from his harem.

Her throat dried. Was that what this was all about? Did he want to get her accustomed to the idea of sharing him?

Never.

Blond hair winked in the dim light seeping between the cracks of the planks above, a chorus of feminine giggles a fleeting sound in the brisk ocean breeze. Then three shadows solidified into one as the trio lay together on the sandy beach and continued their tryst.

A breathless mewl was followed by a groan, then the sound of skin slapping-on-skin.

Arabelle's cheeks heated and her legs were suddenly shaky. She shouldn't be here. Though it was shadowy and dark it was still too intimate. Too private. Too hot. And yet she couldn't deny having to make use of her other senses—including her imagination—set off her voyeuristic side.

"Our resident backpacker is enjoying himself a little too much," Mahindar murmured thickly.

The blond surfer dude? She stifled a giggle. She should have known.

She exhaled softly. "Is there such a thing as *too much* enjoyment?" she queried in an undertone.

"In this case, yes. Though one of the women is single, the other woman is most definitely married. Clearly not happily married, though."

Yet it was okay for Mahindar to fuck his wife and then return to his harem? She stiffened, all her desire leaking away like water through a sieve.

"We should probably go," he said, as though sensing her sudden objection.

"We should," she agreed stiffly.

He drew her away from the cries and sighs and back toward the pier. It all seemed so incredibly normal again with everything cleared away, with only a string of fairy lights getting taken down.

Most of the villagers had withdrawn, but the jeep driver materialized out of the shadows and asked deferentially if they were ready to return home.

Within minutes they were back in the jeep. Mahindar took off his jacket and wrapped it around her, and she smiled thanks and snuggled into its warm folds, his amber scent wrapping around her.

When the driver pulled the jeep in front of the house, the storm was close with thunder rumbling and lightning crackling across the sky. Arabelle took the time though to lean toward the driver. "Please thank the villagers for a lovely evening."

The driver smiled and assured her that he would, and Mahindar helped draw her out of the vehicle and pulled her close to his side as sketched a wave, and the driver roared off into the night.

Chapter Seventeen

The wind had begun whipping into a frenzy when Mahindar led Arabelle across the ramp at a run, the railing either side buffering them. By the time he'd keyed in the code that unlocked the back door, his wife was laughing hysterically.

He couldn't help but join her. The wild weather drew out something feral and uninhibited, something intrinsically thrilling and elemental.

Still laughing, they ran hand-in-hand through the house and to the glass doors that opened onto the high deck outside. The sky was black, with the moon and stars no longer visible. The sea was an indistinguishable dark blanket but its spray immediately wet them as the surf crashed and thundered to the shore.

He moved behind her and she gripped the railing with an exhilarated shout as thunder boomed and lightning flashed, illuminating the entire beach and ocean for one bright nanosecond.

Desire surged through him and he drew her damp hair to one side and bent to kiss her nape. Her shiver went right through him and he groaned from deep in his chest as he tasted the cool ocean spray on her warm skin.

He could never get enough of his wife, but the raging storm set his lust raging and his dick harder than a pike, his needs as one with the tempest heading their way.

He was undoing the little pearl buttons that ran halfway down her back just as the rain hurtled down. She gasped, as one with the storm, with him and his needs. The dress fell into a sodden pile at her feet, leaving behind only her heeled shoes and her white thong. His dick jerked. De-fucking-lectable!

He unzipped his fly and released his shaft as she kicked aside her designer dress as though it was a rag. His merciless laugh was swept away in the wind and rain, but the savagery of the moment wasn't lost to him. Neither of them cared about anything except to satisfy the relentless needs within.

"Keep your shoes on," he growled. She was the perfect height to fuck in her heels. Not to mention how damn sexy she looked in them without any clothes. He pulled his shoes off and finished undressing while she peeled down her thong so that they were both fully naked to the elements.

The rain pelted against their skin and he cupped her heavy, straining breasts, then rolled her nipples between his thumb and forefingers. He'd been tempted all night to tweak her nipples and suck her unencumbered breasts through the fabric of her dress. Even under the pier when he'd had the chance he'd somehow stayed restrained.

Her head lolled back on his shoulder, her sharp cry piercing through the maelstrom of noise. Another lightning bolt lit up the world, her eyes glowing. He dropped his hands and pushed a finger deep inside her, the welcoming wetness telling him exactly how ready she was.

Widening his stance behind her, he guided his dick to her core, then slammed into her with all the brutal ferocity she craved. Her shriek of encouragement pushed him straight to the brink. Along with their rain-slicked skin, the wind howling around them and the thunder rumbling ever closer, he wasn't holding back.

She met him stroke-for-stroke, her backward thrusts creating a delicious, hot friction that made the cold wetness around them barely noticeable.

His balls tucked up high and he reached between her legs to knead her clit, the magic button instantly making her come while giving him the same luxury. This round might be quick and brutal, the next round wouldn't be. She screamed into the storm and he grunted as his seed poured inside her, his eyes closing at the intense pleasure coursing through him.

He leaned over her, taking a moment to enjoy the warmth of her back on his chest while the rain swept down his spine and plastered his hair to his head. He kissed the side of her neck and she twisted her head a little so that their mouths connected, the kiss deep and lingering.

Another lightning bolt lit up the sky, highlighting his wife's nude perfection, the crack of thunder vibrating the deck underfoot. He caressed her face and gently withdrew from her. "We should probably go inside now."

She didn't object when he bent and lifted her into his arms, then carried her across the deck, through the opened glass sliding doors that led inside the kitchen. He continued into the bedroom without breaking stride.

She giggled. "We're dripping on everything!"

He placed her in the middle of the mattress and followed her down. "Who cares?"

Lightning continued flickering on-and-off, the bedroom lighting up like it was day, then night, then day again. Her eyes gleamed, her small smile filled with humor. "Clearly not you."

"Then you'd be right. I don't sweat the small stuff. I have bigger picture problems to solve."

She tensed beneath him, and he smiled. His smart little wife was overthinking things now. Time to remedy that.

He pressed kisses to her brow, to her eyelids, and then worked on her mouth until she opened up to him and his tongue bumped and danced against hers. Then he was moving down her jaw, her throat, before he concentrated on each of her quivering, heavy breasts, where he sucked her nipples into sharp diamond points.

She gasped. Not good enough. He moved further down, swirling his tongue around her navel and dipping inside. She jerked and moaned. He continued kissing down, pushing her legs apart with his hands then thumbing open her outer petals to the glory within.

Her drawn-out, shuddery gasp when he licked her in one long stroke was music to his ears. But her cry when he focused on her clit was the ultimate grand finale.

He leaned closer. Had she forgotten about the double encore?

Chapter Eighteen

Arabelle drifted in a hazy, orgasm-induced sleep, where very little penetrated the many layers of darkness pressing down on her. But then something niggled and gnawed at her, a sense of urgency that shook her out of her comfort zone then held her in its grip, tearing her through the void.

Her eyelids flicked apart as Mahindar paced back and forth, his cell phone pressed to his ear. She stayed still, silent, as his voice washed over her, masculine, yet clipped and slightly accented. And oh so Sexy.

In that unguarded moment, he reminded her of a wild and gorgeous desert cat, sleek, tough and menacing, but smart and resourceful, too. Few would mess with him.

He stopped, his shoulders as tight as his voice. "It's obviously become a matter of urgency. Just...I'll handle it. Keep me informed." He nodded, a reflex action to affirm whatever it was the person on the other end told him. Then he finished with a curt, "We'll leave within the hour. See to it the jet is ready to go."

He disconnected and her stomach roiled. What on earth was going on? She sensed he hadn't been lying when he'd said he wanted this honeymoon with her to get to know one another. He wouldn't be cutting it short unless it was of utmost importance.

The word *urgency* had been used, a little voice reminded.

"I guess you heard we're leaving?" he asked brusquely.

She blinked and focused on him. "I did," she admitted. "Is something wrong?"

He folded his arms and nodded. "I'll tell you everything on the flight home. For now though, you'd better get dressed. I'll organize someone to pack our things while I make us some coffee and toast."

She nodded obediently, leaving the warmth of bed to drag on soft gray pants and black ankle boots, then a thin cream shirt followed by a gray woolen shawl for the layers that were often needed when travelling. On impulse she clipped on a fine gold choker, which looked lovely against her lightly tanned skin.

She sighed. She'd miss the private beach. She'd miss their privacy, period.

At least they had time for a lingering cup of coffee and hot, buttery toast on the deck while hired staff arrived to pack away their clothes and toiletries.

The dawn sun glinted on the now gentle waves, creating effervescent flashes and sparkles in the water that were almost blinding, the odd whiff of the briny ocean offsetting last night's rain, which had washed everything in a fresh scent. A pelican landed in the water and lifted a wing, using its huge, ungainly beak to preen its feathers.

"I'm going to miss this," she admitted quietly.

"Me too," he conceded. He stood beside her at the railing, and after finishing his toast, he looped his arm around her waist. "We'll be back before you know it."

She smiled up at him. "I'm going to hold you to that."

"I hope you do."

Twenty minutes later she was sitting in the back of the jeep with her husband, whose long, drawn out silence made her a little jumpy for whatever was ahead.

It wasn't until they were finally in the jet winging through the air, another piping hot coffee in her hand, that he told her the bad news.

He sank into the seat next to her, his eyes locking onto hers. "Sweetheart, there is no easy way of telling you this but...Lumana is under attack."

Her heart lurched and for a moment acid burned its way up her throat. *"What?"*

He took away her coffee cup, then clasped her hands. "I know this is a shock, but I'll do everything in my power to reverse the situation. I have strategies in place already and people on the ground working directly with—"

She pulled back. "What about my parents? My mother?"

Though she'd had very little to do with her family over the years, her mother had made the effort to visit at least twice a year. She'd rented a lovely little cottage in London a few miles from Arabelle's university, where they'd often hired bikes and gone for long rides, revisiting places from her mother's childhood. Her mother had spoken wistfully of her dear British friends, who she'd given up when she'd married.

Arabelle didn't want to be like her mother and sacrifice everything for her husband. It wasn't right or fair. Then again, for a lot of women in a lot of countries around the world, life was never going to be fair.

Mahindar searched her eyes, his hands moving to her shoulders. "Last I heard they are both safe. I've sent in some men to retrieve them. But if there is no way out they will guard them and keep them safe."

"Thank God." She took a shuddery breath, then glanced at an air hostess who was clearing away their cups. "I'll have something stronger now, please."

"Good idea," Mahindra said. "Get us both something."

As the air hostess smiled deferentially, then hurried away to fulfill their request, Arabelle asked, "So what happens now?"

"You will be under royal guard at my desert palace. You'll be safer there, away from my city residence."

"And what about you?" she asked, a second wave of fear clogging her throat.

"I'll go to Lumana and sort this mess out."

She stared at him with wide eyes. "You don't seriously think I'll stay behind while you go to my country to save my parents and my people!"

His eyes turned as steely as his voice. "It's not safe for you there now. You're my wife, and I will protect you at all cost."

The air hostess returned with a tray, two glassed of ice and a selection of miniature spirit bottles. Mahindar nodded and chose two whiskeys, and Arabelle gulped down the fiery liquid and set her glass down on the table in front of her, then twisted to stare out the jet's window.

What had Mahindar said at one time? *I'll do everything in my power to never endure another war again.* Yet thanks to his marriage to her another war was exactly what he was going to endure.

His glass clinked next to her empty one, bringing her back to the present. She didn't bother turning to face him when she said numbly, "I was never given a choice in this arranged marriage. At least give me a choice in going with you to Lumana and making sure my parents are okay."

He stiffened beside her. "You already know my answer to that, *habibi,* I'm not risking your life and possibly the life of our unborn child."

She twisted further away from him, her gut hollow. There *was* a possibility she was pregnant right now, which meant she shouldn't be drinking, either. Alcohol was easy enough to forgo, but her freedom...that was another matter entirely.

She swallowed back a surge of resentment and pulled her shawl tighter around her shoulders. What she wanted didn't count. She had no rights. She was an object to be kept behind gilded bars. A broodmare.

So why did she press a protective hand to her stomach and decline another drink? She exhaled slowly. Motherhood might never have factored into her plans but she'd do everything in her power to be a good parent.

The journey seemed to take forever and yet no time at all when her mind was whirling with graphic, horrible flashes of bloodied and mutilated, dead bodies. That her mom and dad's faces were too often superimposed on those same bodies kept her panic bubbling close to the surface.

If Mahindar was aware of her apprehension he didn't show it. He was too busy pacing the corridor, the air hostesses now keeping out of his way as he spoke into his phone, making critical decisions on the fly, literally. Arabelle overheard snatches of conversation; words that made her blood run cold.

Air drops. Informants. Safe houses. Military escorts. Negotiation talks.

It only heightened her overactive mind, and she had to forcibly blank out the rest of his phone calls and empty her mind...of everything. It was a shock then when he placed a strong, black coffee in her hands and said gruffly, "We land in half an hour."

"Thanks," she said in a little girl voice. *Shit.* She didn't want to look and sound...lost. But there was no hiding from her trauma. She'd already lost a brother, one she'd barely known, she couldn't lose her parents, too.

Mahindar crouched in front of her, his dark eyes holding hers. "I'm doing everything in my power to make sure your parents will get through this."

She nodded, and said, "I know."

Mahindar smiled gently, then took the seat next to her. Oddly comforted by his close presence, she leaned her head back and closed her eyes, sipping her coffee gratefully.

It seemed like minutes later he was ushering her out onto the tarmac and toward the waiting helicopter. Its rotors were already spinning, her hair flying at the air currents. Mahindar grinned at her crazy hair, then tipped her head back with a hand, kissing her gently, longingly. Then he kissed her brow and the tip of her ear, and said, "Trust me, okay?"

She nodded, and he bundled her into the helicopter, then took a couple of backward steps after he shut her door and the rotors steadily increased rotation. As the helicopter slowly lifted into the air, he raised his arm in farewell and she pressed her hand to the window before the helicopter swung away and her husband disappeared.

She wouldn't—she *couldn't*—think about the emptiness in her chest.

Chapter Nineteen

The gates swung open, allowing the new Sheikha of Rajhabi access to the desert palace. It might have been déjà vu returning with the long chain of security cars, except this time Arabelle was in the middle vehicle, protected front and back from unseen enemies.

Her driver stopped the SUV directly in front of the palace, and Arabelle nodded politely at the robed servant who opened her door, and who then bowed deferentially as she climbed out.

She was tired, dusty and stressed, and without Mahindar by her side she was also a little overwhelmed. The big, yawning emptiness inside her was becoming as scary as the potential threat to Lumana's borders. Not helped by the desert palace, which loomed in front of her like a dungeon, a prison she'd never escape.

"This way, Your Highness," the servant in robes stated calmly. At least he spoke English, even if it was heavily accented. She'd become so accustomed to the British language that Arabic had all but slipped, half-forgotten, to the back of her mind. He smiled broadly, his teeth white in his swarthy face. "Your luggage will be delivered to your suite shortly."

As she followed the servant to the front doors she noted all the extra guards. Not only was a pair stationed at the front doors with more at the gates, there were half-a-dozen or so soldiers patrolling the grounds.

She shivered. They were probably here as much to keep her imprisoned as they were to keep her safe.

She followed the robed servant who took her down a different gold corridor and past some rooms inside the palace she'd never seen before.

Each room was as striking as the last. She even glimpsed what appeared to be a huge ballroom with a black and white checkered floor, which looked new and far too empty.

She was almost tempted to ask where the harem was located, but the bile that threatened to climb up her throat made her decide she'd rather not know.

They went up a flight of stairs and he opened the door to what had to be the master bedroom suite, and the huge bed she'd soon be sharing with Mahindar.

The servant turned to her with another gleaming smile. "His Royal Highness took the liberty of purchasing you a phone and laptop. I've also left a schedule for your mealtimes, though you might prefer to eat in your bedroom or out on the balcony overlooking your private pool and gardens."

He clapped his hands and a small side door opened. A woman in a colored robe—an abaya—stepped inside. "Your maid, Estelle, is also at your disposal. She will get whatever you need and do whatever you ask, within reason, of course."

"Of course," Arabelle smiled. Otherwise she'd be telling Estelle to organize a ride out of here.

Except you really don't want to leave your husband anymore, do you?

Arabelle frowned at her so called voice of reason. Of course she'd leave him! She wasn't ready for this life as a sheikha. She had doubts she'd ever be ready.

Estelle bowed deeply and Arabelle sighed. This was going to be a long and lonely few weeks—months? She mightn't be ready to be sheikha of Mahindar's country, but she wished with everything she had that Mahindar was here with her now.

"Your Highness," Estelle murmured respectfully, I am honored to serve you. If I can offer you any assistance, please let me know."

Arabelle smiled politely. "Thank you, I will."

The male servant pointed to a button inserted into a corner of a desk further away. "You can buzz for Estelle any time, day or night." He bowed then. "Unless there is anything else, I will leave you now. I'm sure you are relieved to be home."

Home? Arabelle looked around at the opulence. It seemed surreal knowing this was the bedroom suite she'd be sharing with Mahindar. It wasn't the same bedroom she'd used while she prepared for their wedding day. This was much grander.

Crimson and gold walls featuring huge mosaic framed pictures, thick plush carpet underfoot and high raked ceilings overhead. The handcrafted bed was huge, bigger than a king-size, its masculine lines screaming of sex and making her wonder how many of his harem women he'd brought here.

Bile threatened and she sucked in some deep breaths to dispel it. Most other woman would be singing high notes at their good fortune, but *this* wasn't home. She wished instead to be walking down the streets of London, laughing with her friends while the delicious scents of pub food wafted in the air.

"Just one thing," Arabelle murmured.

The male servant paused. "Of course, Your Highness."

Arabelle focused on him. "What is your name?"

"Raheesha."

Well then...thank you, Raheesha, for your assistance today."

"I'm glad to be of service, Your Highness. Day or night."

It wasn't until he left that she turned to Estelle and said, "I think I'll have a shower and a lie down."

"Allow me to help you undress and lay out your evening attire."

Arabelle shook her head. "No, thank you. I prefer to do those tasks on my own." At the woman's shocked face, Arabelle added, "I would enjoy an early dinner though out on the balcony."

Estelle's lovely face broke out into a smile, her nut-brown eyes crinkling at the corners. "Of course, Your Highness. Any requests for dinner?"

Arabelle nodded. "Actually, yes. Something...British."

Estelle's eyes flashed disapproval, but she covered it well as she bowed and said, "As you wish," then withdrew from the suite, as quiet as a shadow.

Arabelle picked up the new cell phone, surprised to find her contact list had not only Mahindar's number, but her mom and dad's, too. She rang all three, not surprised when none of them even connected. One of the first things to go in war was power and phone connectivity.

There was nothing she could do from here and she'd never felt so helpless or inadequate. Not even a shower improved her frame of mind. But climbing into bed, with Mahindar's faint amber scent filling her nostrils, she hugged one of his pillows and inhaled deeply, taking comfort from his familiar smell and falling into a deep sleep.

It was the clink of cutlery that woke her a few hours later. The scent of roast lamb dragged her fully awake.

She sat up and blinked. Through the opened glass sliding doors she could see Estelle setting the balcony table. The servant stepped back inside and smiled. "Your Highness. You woke just in time. Your lamb roast with vegetables is served. If there is anything else—"

"No, thank you. You may go now and...retire."

Arabelle resisted snorting. She'd have to get used to the right words to use for servants.

But if Estelle thought her word choice odd, she didn't let on. She bobbed her head and said, "I'll see you in the morning."

Arabelle smiled wryly. "I'm sure you will." She glanced at her luxurious prison. "It's not like I can go anywhere."

Estelle's gaze turned speculative, her eyes glinting oddly. But then the woman smiled shyly, her voice full of understanding as she said, "You will be happier when His Highness returns."

Arabelle nodded, and looked down at the huge bed that dwarfed her. "I will," she acknowledged. Looking back at Estelle, she was surprised to find she'd already disappeared.

Chapter Twenty

The next four days became something of a routine. She had breakfast on her balcony, then swam for an hour in the lap pool before taking a shower and exploring the huge palace. She needed a GPS to find her way around after getting lost a couple of times in the maze of rooms and corridors.

She ate lunch on the balcony, then religiously rang the three numbers on her contacts list. Nothing. After lunch she wandered into the massive library and lost herself in books for the afternoon. The last three nights she'd then followed the lush scents into the huge industrial kitchen, where she watched the hustle and bustle of the cooks and chefs.

Not tonight, though. She sensed how uncomfortable she made the kitchen staff and decided to instead wait for Estelle to bring her dinner once again. Afterwards Arabelle planned to go to the cinema she'd found yesterday. Estelle had already organized the latest blockbuster to watch that night.

She smiled as Estelle stepped through the glass doors onto the mosaic-tiled balcony. What would she have done without her? Estelle had proven herself indispensable in so many ways.

Estelle set the tray down. "The chef thought you might enjoy British food again tonight."

Arabelle smiled and inhaled the heady aroma of a meat pie, gravy and potato mash. "Thanks Estelle, I appreciate everything you've done for me last few days."

Estelle ducked her head, looking more embarrassed than pleased. "It's what I'm here for. I don't expect praise for something I'm trained to do."

"You *should* expect praise," Arabelle said softly. "I'll make sure Mahindar knows what a blessing you've been, too."

Estelle flushed and backed away. "Enjoy your meal, Your Highness. I'll return in an hour to clean up. I can escort you to the cinema then, if it pleases you."

Arabelle nodded. "I would love that. In fact, why don't you join me?"

The other woman looked shocked. "Watch a movie with you?"

"Of course! It might be fun."

Estelle bit her bottom lip, then relented with an bright, glittery smile. "Sure, I'd like that."

Arabelle glanced at the pool and its lush surround of greenery, where solar lights were beginning to light up and chase back the late afternoon shadows. It was so peaceful on the balcony overlooking this private corner of paradise. It would be even better to share it with her husband.

She frowned. Was she actually missing her husband? She shook of the thought and ate some of her dinner. The meat pie was delectable; it's crust light and flaky, the meaty filling delicious with a faint hit of chili. But something felt...off. Not the food. Just the general vibe.

She pushed her plate of food aside and instead took a swig of red wine. She was being sensitive, and rightly so. She'd heard nothing from her husband or her parents and she was getting more worried every day that went by. She had faith that her husband would be victorious in the end, but how many innocent people might die in the meantime? And how long would he be stuck over there?

Her cell phone abruptly rang and she froze in disbelief, before she pushed her chair back so fast it rocked over and crashed onto the tiles. She ran inside and snatched up her phone.

"Hello?"

Her cell crackled and spat noises into her ear. Then, "Arabelle, it's me, Mahindar."

"Thank God! I've been so worried. What's happening over there?"

"I can't talk long. Just letting you know we've gained control of the borders, with negotiations appearing to be successful."

She clasped her phone harder, almost snapping it. Who else but Mahindar could have handled things so expediently? "And my parents?"

"They're safe. I've placed extra security around their palace in case things go south. But I have every reason to believe the worst is behind us."

"Thank you," she whispered. "For...everything."

"You're my wife, my sheikha; I'd move mountains for you." He exhaled softly, and she could hear the muted sounds of machinery and other voices in the background. "I'm about to board a helicopter to take me home. All going well I'll see you in three or four hours."

"You're really coming home," she repeated, all the tension from the last handful of days leeching out of her. "I was starting to think I'd never see you again."

"Nice to know you've been missing me," he teased, though even with the crackling of the phone she sensed his undercurrent of seriousness.

"I never said that," she hedged.

"You didn't have to." The phone snarled something high pitched in her ear before he added, "I can't wait to see you. Knowing you've been sleeping in my bed and I haven't been there making love to you morning and night...it's been torture."

A shiver of need shot down her spine to her toes. "No prizes for guessing what you want when you get here," she murmured huskily.

He chuckled darkly. "Wait for me in something sexy...or better yet, nothing at all." He cleared his throat, his voice a little harder to hear. "I'm so hard I'm ready to explode."

She giggled, her breasts growing heavy and everything within clenching. "Then you better hurry up and get home."

"Oh, I intend to, Princess." The phone crackled and spat again, and his voice changed timbre as he added, "I think I'm about to lose reception. But just so you know, your parents should have full phone coverage in the next few days. They're working on fixing—"

She clutched at her phone as his voice cut out completely. Though she knew he was gone she couldn't help but ask, "Mahindar, are you there? Talk to me." All she wanted now was to keep hearing his voice and to hold onto the news he was coming home.

When she finally put the cell phone down and turned around, she was surprised to see Estelle behind her. "*Shit*. Estelle, you frightened me."

Estelle didn't apologize, just watched her with shining eyes. "His Highness is coming home?"

Arabelle smiled. "Yes. He'll be here in three or four hours."

Estelle nodded slowly. "That is great news."

"It is," Arabelle said in a croaky voice.

Estelle smiled. "We should celebrate. Allow me to take you to the cinema now."

Arabelle plucked at her pale pink dress, which draped to mid-thigh. She hadn't yet gotten used to the idea of dressing in Arab clothes. She'd been too young to remember wearing the traditional robes, though she imagined they'd been cool and comfortable. "I'm not sure I'm in the mood for a film now."

A scented bubble bath and a nice wine might instead be in order.

Estelle's face crumpled. She was clearly crestfallen. "Really?"

Arabelle blinked. "You *want* to watch a movie with me?"

"I would love to! I didn't grow up here. I never really had the chance to experience many of the western pleasures that my new friends indulged in."

Arabelle immediately sympathized with Estelle. She'd clearly been restricted in what she'd been allowed to do. "Then of course we'll go."

Estelle's face lit up. "Really? Oh thank you, Your Highness."

"Please, call me Arabelle. At least in private."

Estelle nodded. "Of course...Arabelle."

Stepping inside the cinema was like stepping back into the western world. Though a robed usher stood waiting for them from the corridor, once he led them inside the darkened room and asked if they'd enjoy a bucket of popcorn and lemonade, Arabelle forgot about everything but the movie.

The velvet curtains split apart to reveal the screen and the opening soundtrack theme of a major movie production company, the music blasting from hidden speakers around the room. The usher returned with their popcorn and drinks and Estelle said in an aggrieved mutter, "Don't disturb us now until the movie is over."

The usher glanced at Arabelle and she nodded. "Yes, we'll be fine now, thank you." The last thing she wanted was to be hovered over by the usher and interrupted in the best parts of the movie.

She was soon lost in the opening car chase as she stuffed some salty popcorn into her mouth and washed it down with lemonade. She'd always loved going to the cinema, enjoying anything from the last blockbuster to the classics. She turned to Estelle. "Amazing, right?"

Estelle's wide eyes left the screen for a few seconds to look at Arabelle. "You might get me addicted," she confessed.

Arabelle giggled. "Good. I can see a lot of movie watching in our future."

She looked back at the screen. It would have been nice to have seen her first film here with her husband, but she imagined she'd be alone often enough in the future that she'd need a friend to watch some screenings, and Estelle now fit that bill perfectly.

Perhaps it was the thought of her husband being absent all too often, or perhaps it was that niggling sixth sense that many people have that took her out of the movie and made her more self-aware. *Whatever.* She wasn't totally oblivious when someone clapped a hand over her mouth from behind.

She struggled and kicked, her drink and popcorn flying. She tried to scream, but the callused hands were immovable and were soon replaced by a gag stuffed into her mouth. Then a blindfold went around her eyes, too.

Holy shit. Where were the extra guards? What was going to happen to her? A sob welled in her chest with nowhere to go. Would she ever see Mahindar again?

Even over the cinematic sound she heard frantic whispers in Arabic, though she understood snatches of the conversation.

"Hurry."

"No time—"

"If we get caught—"

"Bribed one of the guards—"

But then all sense of perception fled when she realized Estelle was one of the captors whispering furiously.

Arabelle resisted whimpering when her wrists were cable-tied together, but she couldn't help but cry out—a muted and muffled noise—when she was jerked roughly to her feet and tugged unceremoniously after one of her captors.

She banged her shins into a chair, and her captor swore furiously as she fell. He dragged her up by her hair and slapped her face so hard her ears rang and blood trickled from her nose. "Get up, dog," he said in crude English.

She realized then they wanted her out of the palace before the movie ended and the alarm was raised. She'd need to do whatever was necessary to slow them down. She pretended to get up, but stumbled and fell back to the floor.

Her head snapped back as her captor punched her face, the impact almost knocking her senseless as blood sprayed from her nose this time and ran freely down her face. She barely had the strength to function let alone think, her heart beating furiously in her chest.

Self-preservation kicked in. They would kill her if she resisted. She staggered to her feet and followed them blindly, her heart hurting knowing she'd trusted Estelle so easily while constantly resisting her husband's charms.

You wouldn't be here now if your husband had listened to you and allowed you to go to Lumana with him.

She was jerked to a stop, and despite her gag someone clapped a hand over her mouth. It was Estelle who leaned close and whispered, "Make one sound, even a squeak, and you're dead, Arabelle." She laughed so softly it was almost undetectable. "You don't mind if I call you *Arabelle* now, do you?"

Fury burned through Arabelle's veins, but she wasn't stupid enough to act on the emotion. This wasn't the time or place. Except...if she waited too long she'd likely die anyway. These people were utterly crazy to attempt her abduction, which also made them highly volatile and dangerous. They were risking life and limb to take the wife of one of the greatest sheikhs of all time.

But why? What had she done to deserve this?

Then it hit her. These were part of the rebels who'd taken over her dad's borders. The same borders that had been wrestled back thanks to Mahindar's power and support.

Shit. In her captors eyes she was at fault. She was the daughter of their enemy. She was also now the wife of the sheikh who'd defeated the rebels and created a treaty that must have been too good to resist.

Clearly not everyone was happy with the treaty.

"Get going," Estelle whispered coldly, then gave her a brutal shove that sent her flying forward and landing heavily onto her knees. She was hauled to her feet by her hair, a whimper building in her throat at the pain that burned through her scalp. Then she was shoved forward once again, turning right and then left, the constant twists and turns leaving her dizzy and disoriented.

Until she was forced to stop and a door slid closed behind them. The sensation of falling followed by a ding let her know they'd boarded an elevator. In all her wanderings inside the palace she had never once seen an elevator. She shivered. Where were they taking her?

"Move," one of the men said gruffly.

She did as he asked and he didn't forcibly shove her forward. A hysterical laugh threatened to bubble up her throat. She suspected she was safer with this male captor than she'd ever been with Estelle.

Oh how easily fooled she'd been by the woman. Estelle had never wanted to be her servant or her friend. Quite the opposite. But at least now the odd expressions that had flitted across Estelle's face made sense. Perhaps if Arabelle hadn't been fretting so much over Mahindar's absence and her parents' welfare she would have paid more attention to her intuition.

Stale air filled Arabelle's lungs, their footsteps echoing eerily as they walked across what she presumed was a concrete floor. She blinked behind her blindfold, petrol and fumes a faint scent in the air. Was this an underground carpark? Did Mahindar keep his cars underground and not at the back of the palace like she'd suspected?

The faint clunk of a vehicle unlocking its doors via a key fob answered her question. It made sense. Mahindar was known for his car collection. They would be safer underground than anywhere else. She swallowed hard. She, on the other hand, had never been less safe. Once she was inside the car there was little chance she'd escape from her captors.

"Put this abaya on over your dress," Estelle ordered. "The hijab should also help to conceal who you really are."

Arabelle ignored Estelle's rough handling, her thoughts instead consumed by the fact these people had planned her abduction to perfection. That she'd fallen for Estelle's disappointment at not seeing the blockbuster movie sent a sickening wave of stupidity through her. The film had given her captors at least ninety minutes to make a getaway.

"Get in," Estelle said viciously, before pushing Arabelle's head down and shoving her onto a seat. "Onto the floor," she added spitefully.

Arabelle clearly didn't move fast enough. Within seconds she was dumped onto the floor, where she landed heavily behind the front seats. The jolt hurt her stomach, and panic swelled. She'd been doing everything possible to protect herself and possibly her unborn child. But now that she was stretched out across the floor, the doors clunked shut and two sets of boots pushed into her back, forcing her further down.

She couldn't breathe and panic was uncontrollable now. She was gasping for breath and was only half-aware of the vehicle starting, then accelerating forward. The vehicle slowed again and then stopped, Arabic words flowing over her.

She wanted to scream out, to warn the guards she was in the car, but the gag made communication impossible, her captors' boots pushing down on her all the harder. She couldn't breathe and suffocation seemed imminent. Her ears rang and panic swamped her.

Then...nothing.

Chapter Twenty-One

Arabelle woke to a guttural, and panicked male voice. "Get the gag off her before she chokes! If she dies we've failed. And we've gone through all this shit for nothing!"

It took her a moment to realize she'd understood every Arabic word.

Rough hands grabbed her, pulled her up and shoved down her gag, sending her hijab askew. She sucked in a breath, the fresh air flooding her lungs and making her dizzy.

"Ugh, she's bleeding everywhere." Estelle's voice oozed with contempt and disgust, as though it was Arabelle's fault she was injured and bloody.

"Then clean her up. The last thing Sheikh Ramirez wants is blood stains in his private jet."

Arabelle stiffened at the name, her blood running cold. *Holy shit!* She'd been so wrong. This had nothing to do with the sheikh of the country bordering Lumana, the same sheikh who'd caused strife and threatened her motherland with war. No. This was all to do with the elderly and vengeful husband of Aisha.

Sheikh Ramirez must have somehow found out about Mahindar's involvement in protecting her.

"Pass me the water canteen," one of the men said gruffly. "I'll use her blindfold as a rag."

Relief was as thick as a blanket as her blindfold was loosened, then taken off her face. She blinked, then squinted against the dazzling flashlight that lit up her face. Her eyes needed time to adjust after going from the semi-darkness of the cinema to the complete blackness of the blindfold.

When she finally managed to flutter her eyelids completely open the shadowy faces of her captors swam in front of her. Estelle's first, then the swarthy, male face of her companion, Raheesha.

Her stomach sank. Of course the male servant who'd met her at the gates would be in cahoots with Estelle. They had probably planned this whole kidnapping thing together.

"Why?" she asked weakly.

He chuckled as he wet her blindfold with some of the canteen water. "Don't play the innocent victim with us." He dabbed at her face, the water stinging a deep cut. "Your western influence hasn't just corrupted Sheikh Mahindar, it threatens to corrupt every woman in this country and its surrounds. Aisha has corrupted far too many already."

Arabelle's head spun. "Aisha can't be blamed for fleeing a cruel madman."

Estelle's breath hissed, her contempt clear. "Sheikh Ramirez is going to have fun torturing you before he trades you for his stupid bitch of a wife. Perhaps for my loyalty in bringing you to him he'll allow me to watch every second of your pain and degradation."

It was strange how much hurt Estelle's comments generated. What had Arabelle ever done to Estelle to make her hate her this much? If this was how Estelle treated those who were nice to her, Arabelle hated to think what happened to those who treated her badly.

"Cool it, Estelle," the driver said smoothly.

Estelle's face tightened. "My skin crawled having to pretend I was friends with this lowlife dog who chose a western culture over her own!"

The driver looked into the rearview mirror, the dash lights revealing enough of his dark stare to show it was empty of emotion. "I think she's more than aware of your revulsion now."

Arabelle narrowed her eyes. She wasn't stupid enough to rile them, but she was pushed enough to tell the truth. "I did *nothing* to deserve any of this except fall for a friendship that was never there."

"You were blinded by your titles and wealth," Estelle gritted out.

"Titles and wealth mean nothing to me," Arabelle refuted.

"Liar!" Estelle screamed.

"Enough!" the driver snapped. "She will be in Sheikh Ramirez's hands soon enough, and we all know how that will end. Ramirez is fully aware that hurting her will hurt Mahindar worse than anything else."

"She blinded our sheikh," Raheesha agreed quietly. "She is a witch."

Arabelle heaved a fitful sigh. So she was no longer a dog, then? She supposed that was an upgrade, at least.

It didn't make their treatment of her any easier to bear. Her whole face was swollen and inflamed, the cuts stinging and her bruised flesh aching. At least her nose was no longer bleeding.

Arabelle managed a snort. "Are you forgetting Mahindar's influence and power? He will destroy you—*all* of you—for abducting and hurting me."

Estelle's eyes flashed before she struck Arabelle with an open hand, the *crack* heightened somehow by the ringing in her ears.

"Enough!" It was the driver again who intervened. He twisted to glance at Arabelle and warned, "One more word out of your mouth and my people will take great pleasure in shoving a gag back in." He looked ahead again. "Estelle, this is your last warning. Do not touch her again. You've had your fun. But Sheikh Ramirez wants the privilege of torturing her. He will be furious you have already marked her."

Whatever fight Arabelle had in her died a sudden death at hearing her fate. If Aisha had to runaway thanks to his cruelty, what would he do to a woman he considered an enemy?

She blinked back tears, which only made her face hurt all the more. She looked down at her wedding ring, the gold band with its embedded, shiny diamonds distracting her from the dark thoughts threatening to overpower her.

Her marriage had been short and fraught with tension, but it had been a good match while it had lasted. She just wished she'd given her husband more of a chance. He was a good man, a wonderful husband and generous lover. That it had taken this nightmare for her to fully realize that was nothing less than another fist to the face.

She looked out the front windshield, where blazing headlights showcased the desert landscape of sand and dunes, and the rocky embankment either side of the road that was barely more than a faded track. How long had she been gone now? It felt like ten hours but she imagined it had been at closer to three or four. The guards would be alert now to her disappearance. Mahindar had probably also been informed by now.

Her pulse stuttered. She only hoped he had some kind of plan. Anything to get her out of this mess before it was too late.

Estelle and Raheesha began to converse in low voices, when the driver shouted, "Quiet!"

Thwick. Thwick. Thwick. Thwick.

Arabelle closed her eyes at the familiar and escalating noise, hope a shaft of light that poured right through to her soul.

She forced her eyes back open, the red flashing lights in the night sky all too visible as two helicopters approached.

The driver accelerated with a curse. "How the fuck did they find us?"

Estelle's voice shook. "We took all the back roads!"

"Shut up!" the driver barked. "Check your weapons."

The closest helicopter swooped so low it had to be just a few yards above the SUV's roof, the noise and force of its rotors shaking the vehicle. The driver cursed again and swerved, almost running off the goat track of a road and into the rocky embankment to one side.

Raheesha quickly checked his gun, then dragged Arabelle close and murmured thickly, "If we die, you die."

There was nothing she could say that wouldn't make matters worse. Instead she kept silent and her eyes on the road ahead. It was only when the helicopter dropped onto the too-thin strip of road and faced their way with a blinding spotlight that the driver snarled out some Arabic curses and slammed his foot on the brake.

Estelle looked behind them, her eyes wild and voice panicked, "We can't turn back. The other helicopter has landed behind us!"

"They've closed us in," the front passenger growled in heavily accented English.

Estelle's eyes shone. "They'll kill us all."

Raheesha put his arm around Arabelle's neck, his grip tightening. "Not before I kill Mahindar's precious sheikha."

She was wheezing for breath when the driver roared, "Don't kill her you fool, not yet! We might need her."

"We *don't* negotiate," the man said in the front passenger seat. "Not with—"

"Shut your mouth." The driver glowered, his eyes merciless. "We do whatever we must to survive. If any of you try to be a hero I'll shoot you myself. Got it?"

They all nodded in deference to the driver, and Arabelle's mind ticked over. He was clearly in command. But who was he in relation to Ramirez? Was he one of his advisor's? A high-ranked soldier?

He clearly wasn't someone she wanted to fuck with because his authority was absolute, even with his gang of rebels.

Though one of her eyes was almost sealed shut thanks to her rough handling, Arabelle's good eye saw the helicopter door opening and the silhouette of someone climbing out. He half-bent beneath the rotors as he walked. Then he straightened and strode unhurriedly toward them.

Like he had all the damn time in the world.

Mahindar.

That he was fully robed made him look all the more impressive. And even with his keffiyeh headwear she'd now recognize him anywhere. He was a sheikh through and through. Power fairly radiated from him.

Her pulse accelerated. If she'd once thought of him as the devil she'd swear he was now her avenging guardian angel, hell bent on retribution. She shivered. He was looking out for his own, and she was most assuredly *his*.

Even the driver paled in comparison.

"What should we do?" Estelle whimpered, her shaky hands barely keeping a grip on her gun.

"You will all wait here." The driver snapped off his seatbelt and opened his door. "Sit tight for now and don't do anything unless I signal otherwise. You know the drill."

Chapter Twenty-Two

Mahindar had never experienced such a violent need for vengeance. That his wife—sheikha of his peaceful country—had been taken from the very palace and home where she was meant to be safe, had sent wave upon wave of emotions running through him. Rage. Fear. Guilt. Then all three simultaneously.

His wife was innocent, nothing more than a pawn to be used against him. Mahindar's gut tightened as he strode toward the SUV and its driver stepped out. The man lifted one hand to soften the glare of the spotlight while his gaze swiveled cautiously as he walked slowly toward Mahindar.

Mahindar's eyes narrowed. He didn't recognize the man. He glanced at the dark windows. Arabelle was inside the vehicle somewhere, there was no disputing that. He was only glad he'd had the foresight to install a miniscule tracking device inside her wedding band.

It didn't mean she was unhurt, though.

Fury pulsed through him like a dysfunctional electric current. If they'd touched even a hair on her head there would be hell to pay.

He stopped halfway and waited for the sniveling coward to meet him. His lip curled at seeing the gun in the other man's hand. But he didn't react. He needed all his wits if he wanted to play his cards right and win this hand.

Mahindar said nothing as the other man finally stopped in front of him. Only after the man meekly bowed did Mahindar ask, "What is your name? And what is it you want with my wife?"

The man's swarthy skin went a sickly shade of pale. "I am Ahmed. I've been tasked to bring home Sheikha Aisha by kidnapping your wife and making a trade."

His gut instinct had been right. His wife's kidnapping had had nothing to do with her father's enemies. His chest tightened. The enemy was all Mahindar's and he'd unwittingly dragged his wife right into the thick of it. Despite his angst he kept a steely face. "If Sheikh Ramirez knows where Aisha is hiding, why bother with this trade?"

"He doesn't know exactly where she is," Ahmed admitted. "He just knows you have her hidden somewhere on your island."

Bloody hell. It would only be a matter of time before Ramirez found her. Taking Arabelle in the meantime was simply the vicious sheikh's way of saying *fuck you.*

"And how did he come by this information?"

Ahmed's mouth tightened. "I can't tell you that. Not without some kind of assurance I won't be hurt or killed."

Mahindar's mouth curled. Ahmed wasn't worried about his foot soldiers getting hurt or killed. He was worried about saving his own skin.

"I won't have you torn apart by my helicopter's cannons if you tell me who the traitor is that reported Aisha's whereabouts to Ramirez."

Ahmed stayed silent for a good ten seconds, as though weighing up his options. When Mahindar stayed silent and resolute, Ahmed reluctantly nodded. "It was a man going by the name of Shawn."

"Shawn?" It was a western name. One Mahindar wouldn't have forgotten if he knew the man.

"Tall. Blonde. Green eyes. He's been staying at your island village under the guise of a backpacker."

Fuck. It all made so much sense now. Arabelle had said Aisha's name and the man—Shawn—had heard every word.

Though Mahindar remained outwardly calm, Ahmed must have sensed the ruthless impatience bubbling within. If Ahmed truly comprehended half the depth of Mahindar's emotions the man would have pissed his pants by now. Mahindar held the other man's nervous gaze. "I want my wife. *Now.*"

The man swallowed. "As you wish, Your Highness." He cleared his throat. "Just don't be shocked when you see her."

"When I *see* her?" Mahindar growled. Ahmed's choice of words only heightened Mahindar's already dark emotions into something even darker.

The man nodded, his eyes downcast. "My companions got a little rough with her. I *did* stop them though—"

"Get. Her." Mahindar's voice throbbed with fury. If wrath was a bird, then his was an eagle, its talons outstretched and wings folded back for the kill. He nodded at the two helicopters, front and back. "And just so you're aware, those cannons I mentioned are trained on you right now. If my wife is manhandled from this point on, you *will* be blown to pieces."

Ahmed bowed once again, his face strained. "Of course, Your Highness. My profuse apologies. I will get the sheikha now."

Mahindar was a skilled negotiator, one of the best, but his heart was in his throat as the other man walked back to the car like a whipped dog. It was all too obvious he was scared shitless of showing him Arabelle.

Mahindar's pulse echoed like a drum in his ears. Ahmed had every reason to be afraid. If Arabelle wasn't the same beautiful goddess stepping out of the SUV he wasn't sure he'd have the willpower to hold himself back.

Ahmed pulled open the door, his voice too fast and low to hear clearly. Then a woman stepped out, her eyes flashing with an equal measure of fear and loathing.

Mahindar's eyes narrowed. He knew that woman!

Estelle.

Son of a bitch. He'd hired her as Arabelle's personal maid. She'd come highly recommended by one of his best friends after she'd worked dutifully at his palace for six months.

His mouth tightened. He'd talk to Fayez about this woman, Estelle. But right now he had to get his wife back. Safe and sound.

Estelle stepped stiffly aside as another woman alighted from the backseat and stood directly in front of the spotlight.

Mahindar's stomach dropped, then hit rock bottom. A flash of stark violence almost brought him to his knees. His wife was bloodied and bruised, one eye closed shut, her bottom lip split and her cheekbones swollen. That this was the same woman who'd dared to flick him and his drone the bird, was probably the only reason she was still alive.

He didn't move, didn't allow them to see how affected he was by his wife's injuries. One thing he'd learned as sheikh was to never give away his emotions.

This was *his* fault. No one close to him was ever going to be safe. His wife included. The proof was right in front of him.

He stalked toward her in a slow and measured stride, his face blank, empty, while his mind spun with sickening images of the vengeance he'd inflict on her captors. His breath shuddered out as he neared her. If he gave into his emotions now he'd most definitely do something he'd regret.

Keeping everything inside him shut down, he stopped five yards away from his wife and said neutrally, "Arabelle. You're coming home with me now."

She didn't say a word as she stepped past her captors and toward him. That she did so with her battered head held high and her spine straight, as regal as the day he'd met her at their wedding, showed she was a sheikha through and through.

His heart wrenched. He couldn't have fallen more in love with her if he tried. If only the look in her one good eye revealed the same emotion toward him.

But she was as distant toward him as ever. An icicle radiating coldness. Not that he blamed her. He swallowed past the lump in his throat, his gaze fastening on the man and woman outside the car and the shadowy silhouettes of the two people still inside it. All of whom had kidnapped and assaulted his wife.

That they'd no doubt done irreversible damage to her, not physically but emotionally and mentally, made up his mind. He looked back at his wife and nodded at the nearest helicopter, his voice harsh, "Go. You will be safe with them."

Her good eye flashed with distress. He winced. He deserved her disbelief. His supposed protection had been what had gotten her into this mess.

It wasn't until after she'd thrown off her hijab, her tangled hair falling free, and she'd climbed into the helicopter, that he headed closer to the car. He had no need for a gun, not with the cannon in both helicopters. "Weapons," he demanded." All of them."

Ahmed's lips thinned as Estelle shook her head and mumbled mutinously, "No."

Mahindar stepped closer to the 'maid' and encircled her wrist with his fingers, lifting her trembling hands and the gun she held. His hand tightened at seeing her bruised and skinned knuckles, the red welts under her fingers. She gasped weakly, the gun falling from her feeble grip.

"Good call," he said, pretending she'd deliberately dropped the gun when they both knew it wasn't true. He looked pointedly at her hand, then bent to pick up the gun. He pointed it at her casually, getting small satisfaction at seeing her stumble back from him, twisting her ankle badly on the edge of a rock and falling on her ass.

Ahmed tossed his gun onto the ground between them and held up his hands. "We don't want any trouble."

Mahindar nodded, then bent to pick up the gun. "Then tell your men to get out of the car."

Ahmed spoke rapidly to the other two men and they opened the doors before reluctantly getting out of the vehicle. Mahindar didn't know the man from the front seat but he most certainly knew the man in the front.

Raheesha.

That he'd been a trusted servant and friend scraped Mahindar's nerves raw. He didn't take such treachery lightly.

But Raheesha didn't look at Mahindar, instead his eyes stayed downcast, his face pale and his expression shamefaced.

Mahindar sent them an empty smile. "Toss your guns over the edge of the road."

The rocky embankment on one side hid a cliff that dropped to the ground a hundred yards or more below. Too far for anyone sane to attempt to regain their weapons.

"Do it," Ahmed snarled.

Though resentment flared in the foreign man's eyes, he didn't put up a protest. Neither did Raheesha. They threw their guns, a faint clattering sound echoing seconds later. Mahindar chose to keep Ahmed's firearm, but threw Estelle's gun in the same direction as the others.

Mahindar turned to Ahmed, then nodded at the trunk. "Open it."

Ahmed did as he asked and Mahindar took a look inside. There were two containers inside. One for fuel and one for water. "Take out the water container," he instructed.

The men did so reluctantly, straining and huffing with exertion as they heaved it out and allowed it to drop onto the ground near the vehicle. They stepped back cautiously, their eyes on Mahindar.

"Wait! W-what are you g-going to do?" Estelle asked, walk-hopping toward him.

Mahindar curled his lip at her. That he was tempted to strike her with the butt of the gun must have shown on his face. She stilled, then back-hopped, her complexion paling. That she'd no doubt befriended his wife then set out to hurt her was unforgivable. Such a violent and cowardly act came with a heavy consequence. "I'm doing the least brutal of all the hideous ideas filling my head," he conceded.

Turning back to the water container, he pointed the gun and fired off a shot a little more than halfway down. Water streamed out and disappeared into the sand even as Mahindar stalked around the car and fired off a shot into each tire, then grabbed the keys from the ignition and threw them over the edge of the cliff to join the firearms.

He looked at his enemies with cold eyes. "Though I'd love nothing more than to kill you all now, I refuse to give any of you an easy death. So I'm giving you a choice. Stay here with your dwindling water supply and hope someone shows up on this rarely used road. Or walk into the desert and likely die of thirst. Either way you'll all probably die. It's the least you all deserve."

"P-please. Have mercy!" Estelle begged, tears sliding down her face.

Disgust filled him. "Like you had mercy on my wife? Like you didn't know the torture Ramirez would have devised for her before he likely killed her? Believe me...you are lucky to get off so easily."

He walked away then, Estelle sobbing to the background of hissing air and slowly running water.

Chapter Twenty-Three

Arabelle couldn't look at Mahindar as he climbed into the helicopter then instructed the pilot to take them home. Yet there was a mixed sense of foreboding and relief having him back, while his presence filled the cabin and sucked away all the oxygen.

He really was larger than life. Guess that was why she'd trusted him so much. Had imagined she'd be safe thanks to his brilliant foresight.

And yet...she'd all but begged to go with him, and he'd refused. Her freedom of choice had been taken away from her yet again, to her detriment.

She glanced out the window. Her captors stood around their vehicle, which had lurched at a weird angle thanks to its blown out tires. But though sympathy for their plight stirred inside her, she quickly tamped it down. They had shown her no empathy at all and had been willing to dump her at the feet of a sheikh who was known for his merciless and cruel nature.

She shivered. The trade-off would never have happened. She would have died a slow and torturous death, killed in direct retaliation for Mahindar hiding Sheikh Ramirez's wife.

That Mahindar's face had showed nothing...no empathy, no concern when he'd looked at her had broken something inside her. She really thought he'd cared about her. Had presumed her suffering would have at least touched him in some way. She'd been so wrong.

Mahindar's big hand enclosed hers and she jerked away from him, her heart thudding hard as shock and fear suddenly coalesced inside her. "Don't." *Please don't touch me. Or I'll break into pieces.* "I'm. Fine."

"You don't look fine," he said gruffly.

She blinked back sudden tears. She refused to cry! Why did he pretend to show concern now? It only made her hate him more!

She turned away from him then, but felt his eyes on her long after her shock and fear had subsided into something manageable. She dragged in a steadying breath. It was only natural after an attempted abduction and horrible assault for her to feel this way. But she was strong. In the coming weeks she was certain it would all seem like a bad dream.

The helicopter began its descent, the palace looming below. She closed her eyes, panic once again escalating. *Stop!* She was safe now. Despite her seesawing emotions in regards to Mahindar, he was by her side now and she was certain he would have tightened his security to epic proportions.

But what of Aisha? Had her despot husband found her yet?

Mahindar helped Arabelle out of the cabin and she ducked under the powerful rotating rotors and followed him from the rooftop helipad and down the stairs into the much cooler palace. Sending her an apologetic look, he immediately lifted his cellphone to his ear and barked out orders.

A handful of his men were to retrieve Aisha, then hold the blond man called Shawn for questioning.

Her blood pressure dipped. The blond surfer dude? A chill slid through her blood. Hadn't he been at the holiday house when she'd mentioned Aisha to Mahindar?

Her husband grimly disconnected the call and Arabelle finally spoke, though her words seemed to stick in her suddenly thick throat. "It's my fault. I should never have mentioned Aisha."

"It's no one's fault," Mahindar growled. "I should have moved her off the island a long time ago." He exhaled heavily. "Regardless...my men know what to do. Aisha will be safe."

Arabelle breathed a sigh of relief, then asked, "How did you know where to find me?"

He stiffened a little, then conceded, "I had a tracking device inserted into your wedding ring."

Her pulse stuttered. "So you knew I was never safe here?" she asked bitterly.

His face tightened. "You're a sheikha. That puts a target on your head. That you're the daughter of a sheikh who is still teetering on the edge of war makes you an even bigger mark. I put measures into place to ensure I could at least follow you."

He stopped when they reached the floor, then turned to face her as she stood on the bottom step. He still had to look down at her as he examined her face. His eyes were hooded but there was no mistaking the concern. "You were under my protection, *habibi*, and I failed you. For that I will never forgive myself."

Was that his way of apologizing? She might have laughed if everything didn't hurt so badly. Her face wasn't the only thing bruised, cut and sore. Her back ached and no doubt was bruised from the booted feet of her captors and her stomach swirled and pitched like she was going to be sick.

And then there was her heart...

She searched his stare, her one eye seeing all too much. "Then you should have taken me with you." She couldn't stop the lone tear from trickling down her face. "You said I would be safe. But you were wrong. I would have been safer if I'd been with you."

His expression gentled as he carefully thumbed dry her tear. "You're right," he conceded. "I never factored in Ramirez. Let me have my doctor check you over then—"

"No. No doctor," she interjected. "Not right now." She bit her bottom lip, and winced. "I need you."

He blinked down at her. "You're hurt and probably in delayed shock—"

"You'll be gentle with me," she insisted. She had no idea why she needed him physically after all she'd been through, but she craved him like she was a sex addict who needed her fix. "Please," she whispered, as close to begging as she'd ever get.

He groaned, then bent and scooped her carefully against his chest before he strode toward their bedroom suite. There was something thrilling about all his power. Not just as a leader of a nation. Even in his robes she could feel his strength as he so easily carried her.

He was an incredible man. And though she might tell herself she hated him, her feelings for him went much deeper and more complex than that.

He stepped inside their bedroom and kicked shut the door behind them. In three long strides he then lowered her onto the bed and followed her down.

There was something beyond intimate in slowly undressing one another, and he took his time in taking off her robe and then her dress. That he removed both her western and eastern garb made the ritual somehow even more profound.

It wasn't until she was bared beneath him that his breath hissed out slowly at the dark bruises littering her body.

"It's f-fine. P-please," she said hoarsely.

He bent his head and kissed her throat, her breasts, while one of his hands slipped between her thighs and massaged at that spot that sent her undone so quickly. She moaned and shook beneath him, and he kissed the corner of her lips that weren't split and swollen before he slowly eased inside her.

The joining was exquisite, fulfilling her in a way she hadn't experienced even on their honeymoon. The feeling was poignant and all-encompassing, his eyes glinting with lust and some other, nameless emotion as he watched her while he slowly thrust in and out.

Another tear slipped free and he stilled with a low, savage curse. "Am I hurting you?"

She shook her head. "No. No, of course not." She wiggled a little. "Don't you dare stop now. I *need* this!"

As his assessing, astute gaze finished trolling her face, he nodded and thrust again. His jaw clenched as he held himself back, his eyes glinting and his groan pulling at her from deep inside.

But though he was there, a part of her sensed he was holding something back, an emotional distance that was startling even though her body eagerly responded and was drawing higher and higher toward gratification.

Then he reached down and massaged her clit once again. The string snapped between them and broke away, and she flew high as she orgasmed, her cry long and drawn out, her contracting muscles dragging him along for the ride as his warm seed rushed inside her and his hoarse shout echoed against the walls.

He didn't stay connected though. He immediately withdrew, his forearms bunching to hold his body off hers while he studied her face, as though expecting her wrath or perhaps for her to fall apart emotionally.

She blinked up at him. "I'm not made of glass. I won't break."

"You say that now," he said hoarsely.

He straightened and she watched him retreat to the bathroom. His ass was nothing short of sculpted beauty while his back muscles stretched and released with every step. She sighed, her heart stretching and pulling in a similar way.

I love him.

She sat with a jerk, her hand touching her suddenly cramping stomach. Was it possible to love someone in such a short time? That she'd been so intimate with him had no doubt propelled the emotional response, but even so...

She swallowed. Was it possible her abduction had left her wanting to be loved? Or was she simply open now to the truth? If the kidnapping had taught her one thing, it was that life was too short to stuff around with matters of the heart.

She lifted a hand to her brow. She'd fought against this marriage tooth and nail, but she realized now her feelings for her husband weren't to be taken lightly. She wanted him, desperately.

Her stomach compressed and cramped some more as she pushed off the bed and headed toward the bathroom as Mahindar stalked out, a towel wrapped around his hips.

He glanced at her with another assessing gaze and said, "I thought it might be best to eat out on the balcony tonight. In the meantime I'll get the doctor to take a look at you. You might require stitches and he has the best antibacterial—"

Warmth trickled down the inside of one leg, and with a startled cry she ran to the shower and stepped inside, turning the water on to wash away the first signs of blood. But not before her husband would have noticed her time of month had arrived.

Following her into the bathroom, he opened the glass door as she turned to him with water pouring over her and tears rolling down her face. "We're not having a baby."

Chapter Twenty-Four

It was odd how much those words hurt to say. She'd never had plans for a family and yet now she wasn't pregnant she yearned to carry Mahindar's baby. That Mahindar's face paled at the news only increased her despair.

But despair warped right into devastation when he exhaled heavily and said, "Perhaps you were right all along."

"What do you mean?" she asked, her voice cracking sharply.

"I should never have forced you to marry me. You will never truly be safe as my wife."

The hurt from her captors was nothing compared to the staggering amount of pain that shafted through her like ice picks to her heart. She was clearly too much trouble to keep around. That she couldn't even bear him a child had no doubt cemented his change of mind about her.

His hands clenched the glass door, and she wondered hysterically how it didn't snap. He visibly swallowed as she stared at him, her raw emotions rendering her with so much heartache she was left speechless and barely able to breathe.

"I'm letting you go," he said hoarsely. "I can't protect you, I know that now. And you might still have a chance with that man you love."

She wrapped her arms around herself to still the tremors inside. Hadn't that one lie come back to bite her hard? But she was too proud to admit the only man she'd ever love was the one standing in front of her. When she finally managed to speak next, her voice was surprisingly flat. "So this is it then? We're done?"

His brows pulled in as he nodded sharply. "We're done," he repeated. Then he added vaguely, "I'm only sorry I didn't realize it sooner."

He spun and stalked away, his usual graceful stride now jerky and stiff.

She folded in half and let the tears course down her face, her whole body shuddering. Not only had she lost a brother, she'd lost a husband, too. That she was also denied the privilege of a baby meant she was surely cursed.

The tears came harder. Perhaps shock *had* finally set in. Her legs had no substance and her breaths came out ragged and raw. That she'd never truly grieved for her brother only added to the weight of her grief, her mind twisting with illogical thoughts.

Perhaps she deserved this punishment? She'd hardly known or remembered her brother and she'd never truly appreciated her husband for the decent and wonderful man he was. She'd turned her back on everyone she should have held close.

This outcome was what she truly deserved.

A long and lonely life with nothing more than a career to stave off memories of the man she loved and thoughts of what might have been. Because she knew now without a doubt it was Mahindar in her life or no one.

She sobbed harder. So much for mentally fighting her husband every step of the way and never allowing him to touch her emotionally. She couldn't have fallen for him any deeper.

She swallowed back her grief and straightened, then lifted her tender face into the hot, stinging droplets of water. Like it or not, she needed to be stronger than ever now. She'd gotten her wish of freedom and independence. Now she'd have to suck it up and find a way to fill the void inside.

She had no idea how long she stayed in the shower, but once she blindly reached up for the lever and cut off the water, she was as weak and fragile as spun glass.

But within minutes she was dried and dressed, and staring at her shockingly swollen, black and blue face in the mirror, when a knock sounded on the bedroom door.

Mahindar?

Had he changed his mind? Was he returning to apologize and to let her know he couldn't lose her? Her heart in her throat, she hurried to swing open the door, only to find a robed man waiting for her, a medical bag in hand. She slumped a little, only vaguely aware the man looked English despite his dress code.

He tutted, his blue eyes sharp as they assessed her face. "You really were put through the wringer. Let me take a look at you." He stepped into the suite. "I'm Dr. Smith. I'd say it's a pleasure to meet you but I'm guessing you would rather to have met me in any other circumstance but this one."

She managed a smile and he directed her to sit on the bed while he did a thorough examination. She flinched when he touched her ribs and a couple of other places where she was bruised. Thankfully there were no broken bones. But she required stitches to her bottom lip and he applied antibiotic ointment to her many cuts.

Once the doctor was finally satisfied, he stepped back. "You'll need an ice compress on your swelling and bruises." He took out a little packet from his bag and handed it to her. "You'll need these painkillers, too.'"

Will it help with my heartache?

She shook off the bleak thought and asked, "How long before the swelling goes down and the bruising fades? I have a-a plane to catch."

The doctor frowned at her. "You really shouldn't be travelling in your condition. I'd say it will be at least a week before you're looking close to normal, but the mental trauma could take months, even longer—"

"I want to leave as soon as possible. I-I don't care about anything else."

The back of her nape prickled and she slowly twisted to see Mahindar in the doorway. His lips were thin and his eyes glittering. How long had he been standing there?

He stalked forward, his mouth twisting at the sight of her face. Then his gaze held hers and he said hoarsely, "Don't worry. Everything has been set into motion. You're leaving tonight."

She blinked. He was in *that* much of a hurry to get rid of her? The pain that lanced through her left her dizzy. *"I am?"*

He nodded stiffly. "My private jet is ready and waiting for you. My people are discreet and won't mention your injuries. A counsellor will also be arranged back in England along with a sizeable allowance and expense account."

The backs of her eyes burned. He really couldn't wait to get rid of her! "Keep your money," she said flatly. "I don't want it."

He crossed his arms. "And I want you to have it."

What was she? A problem he wanted to wrap up neatly and put away out of sight. That he was able to discard her in another country must be a blessing for him now.

The doctor cleared his throat. "Well, if there is anything else...?"

"That will be all, doctor," Mahindar said. "Thank you."

The doctor nodded, his sharp eyes returning to Arabelle. "I hope you feel a whole lot better soon."

The doctor made a quick getaway and Arabelle was left staring at her husband. That they would soon be divorced and some other woman would become his wife and bear his children sent nausea climbing up her throat while another round of dizziness had the room do a slow spin around her.

Mahindar dragged a hand over his face. "I'm sorry," he said huskily. Then he added, "For everything."

Not half as sorry as me.

She pressed a hand to her stomach. "I'm sorry I couldn't give you what you wanted."

His face whitened. "That was never my—"

He stepped back and shook his head. "Pack whatever you want to take, clothes, jewelry, shoes. You're driver will be here shortly." He looked down at his feet and then back up to her, his voice cracking as he said, "Take care, Arabelle."

He leaned forward a little, but he didn't touch her. He jerked back and pivoted away. And he walked away from her.

Right out of her life.

Chapter Twenty-Five

Six months later...

Arabelle smiled as she dropped the manuscript to her desk and rubbed her gritty eyes. The first page had drawn her in, but she'd been cynical enough to know too many stories started off great then spiraled downhill from there. Not this one. It had bestseller written all over it.

She looked out her poky office window, with views of the dull alleyway and its dumpsters. Rain smeared the window and muted the already dreary scene outside, but right then Arabelle didn't much care.

She looked down at the wedding ring on her finger. But of course it wasn't there. She'd left her ring on the bathroom vanity where Mahindar would find it. She'd brought nothing with her from that life, except the clothes on her back and the mental scars she hadn't yet managed to shake.

She'd done everything possible to immerse herself in this life and forget about her old life. And this book was the needle in the haystack she'd been waiting for. That she'd already discovered two other bestselling books, one of which was in negotiations for a movie deal, was beyond thrilling.

And she'd done it all without anyone's help.

Scott had of course heard through the grapevine she was back and had offered her a job at his father's publishing house. She'd refused. She never wanted to be dependent on a man.

This publishing house might be boutique, but it was growing fast with many authors hoping to join their team. She was excited to be along for the ride.

She leaned back and stretched, then checked her cellphone. *Shit.* Where had the time gone? Her mother was waiting for her. Arabelle should have met her ten minutes ago for a coffee and lunch.

She sent her a quick text. *I'm on my way.*

After sticking the manuscript in the top drawer of her desk—she was a junior editor with a knack for finding literary gold, she couldn't be too careful—she snatched up her purse and coat and hurried out of her office toward the elevator, giving her co-workers a wave on the way out.

The doors slid shut, closing in on her. Not unlike her life. Her career was all she had now and it stuck in her craw that the one thing she wished for the most was no longer at the top of her list.

She stepped out of the elevator on the ground floor, her lips thinning and her chest aching in its all too familiar way. Was she ever going to get over Mahindar? If time healed all wounds then hers must have been a deep, gaping hole in her chest.

She schooled her features back to neutral as she stepped out onto the wet pavement. The London traffic was horrendous as always but there was a lovely little coffee shop two blocks away, where she was meeting her mom. It had become their favorite little haunt since Arabelle had moved back to London.

Her mother clearly worried about her now, and had visited twice already in the last six months. Not only had her daughter been kidnapped, she was single and alone now, and rejected by one of the world's wealthiest men.

Arabelle was only glad few people recognized her. Mahindar had managed to keep their brief marriage private and un-newsworthy and now she was as faceless and nameless as any of the other eight or nine million Londoners who lived here.

The overhead awnings mostly kept her dry, but the moment the pedestrian sign flashed green for walk, she stepped out into the rain, then slowed and tipped her head back, ignoring the curious looks from passers-by and drivers. This was *her* couple of seconds of freedom to relish.

She'd always imagined choosing her destiny was her freedom. Turned out a career wasn't all creative abandon, there were restrictions, too. She'd learned it was the small things that counted. Such as getting her face and hair wet. Or playing her music loud and dancing in her tiny apartment like she really was wild and free.

She pulled the collar of her heavy jacket up as icy-cold rain trickled down her nape. It was just the reality check she needed. No one was free, not really. Not when bills needed to be paid. She was lucky if she had enough food in the fridge for a week.

Thank God she enjoyed her work and being independent.

She peeled opened the coffee shop door, the strong scent of coffee beans tantalizing her nostrils even as lovely warmth hit her. Her heels clacked across the polished wooden floorboards as she headed toward the rows of tables and chairs where her mother sat.

"Mom," she croaked. "Sorry I'm late."

Her mom stood and embraced her, and Arabelle was enveloped in her mother's exotic perfume. Her mom stood back then with an assessing stare even as Arabelle noted her mom's gorgeous tailored pink coat and blouse, her cream skirt and heels, with the elegant pearls at her neck and ears.

"You look...professional," her mother said, then chided, "and far too thin."

Arabelle looked down at her heavy tweed coat, dark pants and white blouse. It wasn't exactly Vogue, not on her shoestring budget. Her wardrobe was made up of sale items or cheap secondhand clothing. Luckily she had a good eye. "It's a little drab, but serviceable."

Her loss of weight wasn't deliberate. She just found food harder to get excited about these days. It was probably a good thing on her wage. Luckily she was on her way up in her career.

They sat and her mother leaned back with a frown, her eyes flashing with concern. "Your husband gives you an allowance, yes?"

"Ex-husband. And I don't want his money."

Her mother's lips pursed. "You should. He wants to know you're looking after yourself after—"

Her mother cut off whatever she'd been about to say about Arabelle's kidnapping, then asked gently, "Have you signed the divorce papers?"

Arabelle shook her head. "Not yet. I'm still waiting on the paperwork."

"Did it occur to you he might not want a divorce?"

Arabelle's heart crashed painfully against her ribs. "Mom, please! He sent me halfway around the world to get rid of me. I'm under no illusions that he wants me back."

A waitress came and took their order. Arabelle and her mother opted for coffee and a chicken and salad wrap.

At her mother's flushed face and restless hands, Arabelle cocked her head to the side. "What is going on, Mom?"

Her mother looked up a little guiltily, crushing a napkin between her fingers. "Your husband saved me and your father's lives. When I heard of your breakup I was devastated. Your father, too. "

"That was Mahindar's call."

"So why does he look so...broken?" her mother burst out. "He's miserable, darling. Anyone can see he misses you. And with the war that broke out between him and Shiekh Ramirez—"

"There was a war?" Arabelle asked in a scratchy voice.

Her mother nodded. "It was kept under wraps and not well publicized, but it's taken six months for your husband to finally subdue Ramirez and take back control of what was a dire situation."

So he really did start a war to protect his old friend. And no doubt to protect his soon to be ex-wife, too. The ache in Arabelle's chest bordered on painful. Her husband was loyal to a fault, she'd give him that much. "Do you know if Aisha is okay?"

Her mother nodded. "Safe and sound thanks to Mahindar's protection." She blinked shrewd eyes at Arabelle. "But I'm not happy you're alone here and defenseless. I really don't know what he was thinking sending you away."

The emotions that Arabelle had pushed deep down inside her were suddenly set free, a mishmash of fear, shame, sadness, rejection, humiliation and pain. She pushed to her feet, her chair scraping back loudly. "I couldn't give him a baby, Mom. The moment he discovered I didn't conceive was the moment he got rid of me. *That* was all I meant to him!"

"You couldn't be more wrong, *habibi.*"

Chapter Twenty-Six

Arabelle's heart crashed as she looked at the man who'd haunted her dreams every night since leaving Rajhabi. She dragged her eyes from him to stare at her mother. "You knew he was here, didn't you?"

She nodded, her eyes shining with concern. "I'm not blind, dear. You belong together. Not even your career has made you happy without him in your life."

Arabelle swallowed back the sick rage building inside her. "I-I don't believe you two. It's taken me s-six months to rebuild my life and y-you do this!" She waved an arm in the air. "I can't go back. This is my life now!"

She turned and ran past shocked diners, brushing past a waiter with a drinks tray and making the glasses rattle. She kept on running, past more tables and chairs and out the back door. She pushed through it, her legs now weaker than cooked spaghetti.

"Arabelle, wait. Please!"

She spun around as Mahindar stepped outside the alleyway with her. Tears burned the back of her eyes, her throat thick with emotion. How could she hate him beyond all endurance and yet want to throw herself at him all at the same time?

She folded her arms. "How *dare* you come back after all this time and pretend you want me. You can't push me away and then reel me back in. It doesn't work like that! I have a life here, a career! I'm finally happy."

"Are you?" Mahindar asked softly even as he stalked toward her, the rain spilling over him and glinting on his dark hair and shoulders like diamonds. "I wouldn't be here if I thought for even a second you were truly happy. And I most certainly wouldn't be here begging for your forgiveness. You're going through the motions. That's not living, *habibi*."

Habibi. She shivered at the endearment she never thought she'd hear again.

He stopped half-a-dozen paces away from her. "I've been watching you these last few days, Arabelle. I know there is no one you love here in England. I also know you're missing something in your life and that you crave something more."

"Let me guess, that something—*someone*—is you."

"It could be." He arched a dark brow. "I don't need a psych degree to work that out when I see you close your eyes and tilt your head up to the rain or when I see your silhouette through the window as you dance alone in your apartment at night."

He stopped in front of her, his voice both decisive and uncertain. "You wanted your freedom, *habibi,* and you got it. But it's nothing without me, is it?"

"Go. To. Hell."

"I've already been there for six long months. I can't do another month. I can't even do another day. We belong together, Arabelle." He smiled grimly. "Not even your pretend love interest will interfere this time."

The yearning pulsing through her was sending her dizzy. But it didn't stop the bitter anger and resentment she'd suffered all those long months. "You sent me away the moment you knew I wasn't pregnant."

"I did. It seemed like fate after what you endured when I was responsible for your welfare. I couldn't see you hurt like that again. Not ever."

"Yet you didn't even flinch when you saw what my captors had done to my face. You didn't care about me then and you don't care about me now!"

His eyes widened. "You couldn't be more wrong, *habibi*. I was shocked and furious to my core. But I couldn't give away my emotions to those animals who'd captured you. I had to let them believe I was cold and indifferent and that they were the ones who were in danger, not you."

She believed him. There was no denying the raw honesty in his voice. But she wasn't about to give into the hope clawing at her insides. She pressed a hand to her stomach. "So why come back?"

"Because it's taken me this long to realize I can't wrap you in cotton wool. You could as easily get hit by a bus in London's peak hour traffic or hit by lightning as you look up at a storm. Either of those scenarios is far more likely to occur than anyone in my palace having the opportunity to kidnap you ever again."

He scraped a hand over his face, the trench coat keeping out most of the rain from his suit while his dark hair was slicked to his scalp. It only made the angles and planes of his face stand out more starkly. He'd lost weight, too.

"I need you, Arabelle. I did the wrong thing sending you away. All it's done is make me—make us both—miserable."

She glowered, fighting to the end. "I love my job. I'm good at what I do!"

He nodded. "What would you say if you could have me *and* your career?" She blinked at him through the rain and he added, "There is no reason you can't read and edit from Rajhabi. It's safe there now, the war ended."

"My publisher would never agree—"

"They would and they do. They don't want to lose you."

Her pulse pounded in her ears. "Wait. What? You've spoken to them about me?"

He nodded, his eyes darkening at her shrill, accusing voice. But he didn't look apologetic. Not one bit.

"I did. They have no idea I'm a sheikh, only that you're my wife."

"You had no right," she gritted. Yet something inside her was softening, wanting to give into him and his idea.

"Just as I had no right to send you away when you needed me most."

"But you did, didn't you?"

And now it was all too little, too late.

"I did," he conceded. "But in all honesty, I came back that same day to apologize for telling you to leave, and to beg you to stay. Then I overheard you tell the doctor you didn't care about anything else but catching a plane, and all my best of intentions went up in smoke. I thought you wanted to go back to England and to the man you loved."

"The man I'd invented to rub you the wrong way?"

He sighed heavily. "Yes, that one."

She dropped her arms to the sides, much of the fight going out of her. "I only did that knowing you had your harem waiting for you somewhere inside the palace."

"Harem?" He snorted. "Seriously? I had them leave the moment I decided you would be my wife."

Her heart gave a little squeeze. "You did?" she whispered. "So there are no other women?"

"No. Why would I want them when you're all I've wanted from the first day I saw you?"

"I-I don't know what to say."

"Say that you love me." He pulled a box out of his pocket and clicked open its lid, revealing her wedding ring. It was only then she realized he was still wearing his. Then kneeling on the dirty, wet pavement, he said, "I love you, Arabelle. I have from the very first day I laid eyes on you. Take your ring back. Take *me* back. *Please.*"

Whatever doubts and insecurities she had melted away in that moment, disappearing down the street gutters along with the rain. "Yes!" she shouted. She ran to him and he straightened quickly and snapped shut the ring box as she jumped into his arms, his mouth immediately stealing away her breath as he kissed her and she kissed him right back.

Only when she tore her lips free from his did she gaze into his eyes and say, "I love you, too. I denied it for the longest time, but I'm never going to deny it again. We really do belong together." She winked. "And I haven't forgotten that you owe me sex up against the wall."

Epilogue

Arabelle stared at herself in the mirror, admiring the bump of her tummy behind her elegant red evening gown. No birthday present could possibly match becoming a mother. For someone who'd never really thought about children, she wanted a whole posse of them now.

As much as she loved her work she'd gladly scale back her editing to part-time while she raised her baby with Mahindar. He'd been right. Motherhood was surely the most important job in the world, and she wanted to raise her children as best as she could.

She grinned. She was almost certain the promise she'd reminded him about taking her against the wall was when they had conceived. That he'd not used the alleyway walls and had instead waited until he'd taken her back to her tiny apartment was a credit to him.

"You're beautiful, *habibi*."

She turned to her husband, who wore an Armani suit in honor of her birthday. Not that she minded either way. He was gorgeous in both his western attire and his formal robes. It was just a bonus that he wanted to please her.

He strode toward her and placed a protective hand over her stomach as he leaned forward for a long, luxurious kiss. When he pulled back he murmured, "The guests are waiting. But there is just one thing I want to show you first."

She blinked, her curiosity aroused. "Sounds mysterious."

He chuckled and led her out of their bedroom suite and down the stairs. It wasn't until he drew her into the shadowy ballroom and across its black and white checkered floor that she even recalled they had such an expansive room.

"What are we doing here?" she asked in a whisper that nevertheless echoed in the vast space.

"I thought we could have a private dance," he murmured.

She gazed up at him as he turned in the middle of the floor to face her. "Really?"

He nodded. "I'm the first to kick-start the tradition between myself and my three best friends to have a ballroom installed in the palace with checkered flooring. After each of us marries we get to celebrate every important occasion in it with our better halves."

He clapped his hand and a single spotlight lit up a small orchestra in the corner of the room. They broke into a piece of composed music that shivered down her spine even before she stepped into his arms and they glided around the floor alone.

She looked up at him with a smile. "To think I hated dance tuition."

"Mm. To think I hated the idea of installing a ballroom."

She giggled. "Looks like we were both wrong."

He nodded. "I think this ballroom is going to make a great tradition."

"And I'm betting your ballroom won't be the only one we step foot in over the next couple of years."

He arched a brow. "You think all three of my friends will find a wife by then?"

"Of course." She slid her hands down to his ass and squeezed, then added softly, "Every powerful sheikh needs a loving woman to pull them into line."

His eyes glinted. "Then I truly hope they, too, get their happily ever after."

The huge chandeliers above them suddenly lit up and all the birthday guests moved out of the shadowy sides of the ballroom then began to partner up and join them on the dance floor. Even Arabelle's dad pulled his wife into his arms and smiled over her shoulders at Arabelle.

Something in her chest moved. This was the family she'd always wanted. This was what she wanted her children to have.

She grinned at her husband's planned setup, loving him so much it hurt. "You outdid yourself for my birthday."

He winked. "Anything to please my wife."

She looked toward the bar at the end of the ballroom, where one of his best friends stood with a drink in his hand as per usual, and with half his hair dragged into a plaits as though in an afterthought. Sheikh Hamid had the Johnny Depp vibe going on, and his liquid dark eyes looked amused by all the fuss.

She nodded toward him and said, "Hamid is next."

Mahindar threw his head back and laughed. "The day I see him build a ballroom with its checkered floor for his wife—*any* woman—will be the day he actually wants to be a sheikh."

She smiled up at him, and reached her arms up to wind them behind his neck. "Maybe we need to show him what he's missing out on."

Mahindar smiled and said huskily, "Maybe you're right."

When he bent his head and their mouths fused, Arabelle knew without a doubt that being here, with her husband, was the only place she'd ever truly belong.

Want more Desert Kings Alliance stories by Mel Teshco...
The Sheikh's Captive Lover
A sheikh wishing for anonymity. A photographer wishing for great
success.

As a freelance photographer Holly Petersen has never shied away from hard work and a little risk. But traveling alone in the desert in a clunky sedan definitely isn't her best idea. Not when her car breaks down and she's stranded on a goat track in the middle of nowhere with only sand dunes for company.

Until a ruffian on a camel appears from nowhere like an angel from heaven. A pity he's no angel. He's an inebriated devil who expects her complete obedience if she wants to be saved. And staying alone in the desert with little hope of rescue is too much of a risk, even for her.

Hamid Al Wahed was never meant to be the sheikh of his small but prosperous country. That had been his older brother's life ambition before his sudden death thrust Hamid into the role of leader. Having an unlimited supply of booze and women might be its one saving grace, but even that doesn't stop him from craving the solitude he needs by camping out in the desert.

It's there that he stumbles upon a western woman with bright red hair, a death wish and no survival skills , and he realizes he craves even more from his life. And that more is Holly. But first he has to coax her into staying with the fake him...the anonymous savage she imagines he really is.

The Sheikh's Captive Lover available HERE[1]

---

1. https://www.amazon.com/dp/B09KCHKHZV

Chapter one of The Sheikh's Captive Lover

Sheikh Hamid Al Wahed let loose with an elated shout as he pushed his champion camel into a gallop, leaving his mounted guards behind in his dust. Well, sand. Whatever! Nothing right now could contain his happiness. Even his grin had to be eating up his face when one of his random hair plaits caught in his mouth.

He blew it free with another heady laugh. Now this was living!

He'd never be a strait-laced traditionalist. Even wearing the ghutra headdress was a rare occurrence. That it not only protected his face and neck from the desert heat, but also kept his hair covered and out of the way concerned him little. He loved the bite of the sun on his scalp and the wind's hot breath against his skin while his hair was free to do whatever the hell it wanted.

He'd never conformed. He was a full-time ladies' man and a part-time drunk. And a sheikh in name only.

Little wonder his people despaired of him.

The adrenaline rush faded along with his smile, but the desert continued to speed past as his camel galloped up one sand dune and down the next.

Hamid's energy shift happened just as fast as he sank into gloomy thoughts. It was almost laughable that he'd become sheikh of Imbranak via default.

It had been his eldest brother, Ardon, whose role it had been to rule the small but ridiculously wealthy nation. Ardon who had prepared his whole life to become the next sheikh and serve his people...until the helicopter he'd piloted had crashed in the desert, killing him instantly along with his closest guards and advisors.

Hamid have never wanted or asked for the position of ruler. He'd always been a misfit by nature and—when not bedding a beautiful woman or women—a loner by choice. He craved solitude whenever he could get it.

Just like now.

Not even his favorite harem girl, Ranna, could have pulled him out of the despairing funk he'd fallen into once again.

He slowed the camel into a long, loping walk. "Good work, Camille. You've given me some space, if only for a few more minutes." Camille responded with a hoarse bellow and he nodded and said, "Glad you understand. And yes, I am rather thirsty now, thank you."

He pulled a flask from out of his thobe's pocket, then gulped down some fiery mouthfuls of arrak, the date liquor he'd become rather fond of. Though his preference to forget his responsibilities was sex with any number of his women, a mind numbing drink would also do in a pinch.

Both were preferable.

He capped his flask and shoved it back into his pocket. In a perfect world he'd be surrounded by his exotic harem women. In an even more perfect world those same women wouldn't act like puppets trained to remind him exactly who he was at every opportunity.

Ugh. It galled him no end that they spoke his name with such reverence and worshipped him like some ancient deity every time they scraped into a bow or yielded to his every perverted need.

He might love sex but sometimes he really did prefer to be alone in a Bedouin tent in the middle of the desert over the suffocating faithfulness of his servants, advisors, guards and harem women.

That they all resided in his sparkling palace with its gold-plated walls and fountains which gushed water while the sun scorched the barren earth outside its walls, left him with no choice but to occasionally escape where no one could find him.

He might endure the title of sheikh, but he had very little interest in public relations, politics and game playing. It was only his advisors and his surprisingly keen instincts that saw his country continue to prosper.

His lips twitched just a little. Perhaps his best friends, Mahindar, Fayez and Jamal's influence had rubbed off on him? Because, unlike Hamid, they were passionate about ruling and bringing their nations forward like no other sheikhs before them.

His thoughts drifted to his smitten friend, Mahindra, whose mind was sharper than a rapier. When that man wanted something, nothing held him back. Not even a war had managed to keep him away from Arabelle, the woman he loved.

Of course Hamid was pleased for his friend's happiness, but there was a part of him that was a little envious, too. How must it feel to love someone so unconditionally and exclusively?

Hamid had never once freely given his heart to a woman. His preference was to share his love around, or at least, share his body around. But perhaps if the right woman appeared, one who didn't think he was the sun, the moon and the stars because of his sheikh status, he'd reconsider...everything.

He heaved out an aggrieved breath. At least he wasn't alone in being alone. Fayez and Jamal were still happily single. His lips quirked. He had strong doubts either one of them would be building a ballroom with its black and white checkered floor anytime soon.

Hamid still chuckled that his best friends had fallen for his drunken bet a few years ago in a game of blackjack. They clearly thought he'd lose. They might be brilliant strategists and intelligent when it came to advancing their countries, but surely they should have known better than to bet against their street smart and savvy friend?

Had they forgotten about his earlier bet, which he'd also won? It'd been hilarious watching them compete in a camel race in nothing but their birthday suits and anxious faces. That his belly laugh had been far too short-lived had had him thinking up a far more impressive scheme for his next bet, one that would continue for years to come.

Building a grand ballroom for any of them brave or foolish enough to fall in love and marry had come to him after he'd visited a wealthy sheikh with said pretentious ballroom. Hamid had spent seven hours inside that huge room bored out of his skull, the loud orchestra piercing his ears and the overdressed people with their fake smiles and heavy jewelry hurting his eyes.

Thank heavens he'd at least had the good fortune of taking two gorgeous ladies to bed for the night; otherwise the whole experience would have been little better than watching paint dry.

But he'd decided well before those ladies had brightened his mood that his friends should have to go through the same ordeal, and from there his plan had hatched.

Of course his friends had all scoffed at the bet until Mahindar had fallen in love with the one and same woman he pledged to marry. He'd soon after commissioned an architect to build his grand ballroom with checkered black and white flooring.

And without not one word of complaint.

But Hamid was certain his smitten friend would have built a dozen new ballrooms just to be with his wife.

Camille crested the next sand dune with another bellow, pulling Hamid out of his introspection even as a flash of dusty, metallic red caught his peripheral vision. The sedan—a ridiculous choice for driving in the desert—was pulled to the side of the road AKA goat track that snaked around the dunes.

"Just the diversion I need," Hamid announced to his steed.

Taking another glug of date liquor from his flask, he ignored the distant shouts from his guards and pressed Camille into a fast gallop toward the car.

For your exclusive FREE story: Her Dark Guardian, and where you can find out when my next book is available, as well as other news, cover reveals and more, sign up for my newsletter: https://madmimi.com/signups/121695/join

Check out my website – http://www.melteshco.com/

You can also friend me on Facebook at https://www.facebook.com/mel.teshco

Or my author Facebook page at https://www.facebook.com/ MelTeshcoAuthor

And occasionally on Twitter at https://twitter.com/melteshco

Contact me: melteshco@yahoo.com.au

If you enjoy my books I'd be delighted if you would consider leaving a review. This will help other readers find my books ☺

About the Author

Mel Teshco loves to write scorching hot sci-fi and contemporary stories with an occasional paranormal thrown into the mix. Not easy with seven cats, two dogs and a fat black thoroughbred vying for attention, especially when Mel's also busily stuffing around on Facebook. With only one daughter now living at home to feed two minute noodles, she still shakes her head at how she managed to write with three daughters and three stepchildren living under the same roof. Not to mention Mr. Semi-Patient (the one and same husband hoping for early retirement...he's been waiting a few years now.) Clearly anything is possible, even in the real world.

Desert Kings Alliance: series order
The Sheikh's Runaway Bride (book 1)
The Sheikh's Captive Lover (book 2)
The Sheikh's Forbidden Wife (book 3)
The Sheikh's Secret Mistress (book 4)
The Sheikh's Defiant Princess (book 5)
The VIP Desire Agency: series order
Lady in Red (book 1)
High Class (book 2)
Exclusive (book 3)
Liberated (book 4)
Uninhibited (book 5)
The VIP Desire Agency Boxed Set (all 5 books in the series)
The Virgin Hunt Games volume 1
The Virgin Hunt Games volume 2
The Virgin Hunt Games volume 3
Coming soon
The Virgin Hunt Games volumes 4-6
Alien Hunger: series order
Galactic Burn (book 1)
Galactic Inferno (book 2)
Galactic Flame (book 3)
Coming soon
Galactic Blaze (book 4)
Nightmix: series order:
Lusting the Enemy (book 1)
Abducting the Princess (book 2)
Seducing the Huntress (book 3)
Dragons of Riddich: series order:
Kadin (free prequel - book 1)
Asher (book 2)
Baron (book 3)

Dahlia (book 4)
Wyatt (book 5)
Valor (book 6)
The Queen (book 7)
Winged & Dangerous: series order
Stone Cold Lover (book 1)
Ice Cold Lover (book 2)
Red Hot Lover (book 3)
Winged & Dangerous Box Set (all 3 books in the series)
Box sets with authors Christina Phillips & Cathleen Ross
Taken by the Sheikh
Taken by the Billionaire
Taken by the Desert Sheikh
Resisting the Firefighter
Dirty Sexy Space continuity with authors Shona Husk and Denise
Rossetti:
Yours to Uncover (book 1)
Mine to Serve (book 6)
Ours to Share (book 8)
Standalone longer length titles: (50k-100k)
Mutant Unveiled
Shadow Hunter
Highest Bid
As I Am
Existence
Standalone novellas and short stories: (15k-35K)
Identity Shift
Moon Thrall
Blood Chance
Carnal Moon
Stripped
Clarissa

Camilla
Selena's Bodyguard (also part of the Christmas Assortment Box)
Anthologies:
Down and Dusty: The Complete Collection
The Christmas Assortment Box
Secret Confessions: Sydney Housewives

Lightning Source UK Ltd.
Milton Keynes UK
UKHW010932060223
416537UK00002B/572